PLAIN JANE
EVANS
AND
THE
BILLIONAIRE

MALLORY MONROE

AUSTIN BROOK PUBLISHING

VISIT

www.mallorymonroebooks.com

OR

www.austinbrookpublishing.com

OR

www.amazon.com/author/mallorymonroe

for more information on all titles.

ALSO BY

MALLORY MONROE

THE RAGS TO ROMANCE SERIES:

BOBBY SINATRA: IN ALL THE WRONG PLACES

BOONE & CHARLY: SECOND CHANCE LOVE

PLAIN JANE EVANS AND THE BILLIONAIRE

ALSO BY MALLORY MONROE:

ROMANCING MO RYAN

AND

MAEBELLE MARIE

TABLE OF CONTENTS

CHAPTER ONE

Now they loved her. At least that was what they were telling themselves. That they loved her. That twelve years of their sadistic behavior came down to now, on the eve of her departure, as they sat around their dining room table pronouncing their love for her.

Janet Evans sat around that table, too, and listened as the Henleys of Cope County, Oklahoma went on and on about their "affection" for her. From the father to the mother to the daughter and son, they all insisted they were the best thing that ever happened to her and leaving them would be the biggest mistake of her life. They spoke as if she would be leaving paradise. She felt as if she was leaving prison.

They took her in when she was six years old after her kind-but-old foster mother died and the State determined that her kind-but-old foster father was too ill-suited to care for a six-year-old little girl. And back then Janet was so small she looked like she was three. "He wouldn't know what to do with a fragile little girl like you," she remembered one social worker telling her. "If his temper riled up and he put a belt to you, he could harm you something terrible," she also said, which even back then was ludicrous to Janet. Mo Riley, her then-foster-father, was the sweetest man on the face of this earth. He wouldn't harm a flea.

But they wouldn't listen to a six-year-old who'd only been in Mo Riley's household for two short years after her last foster parents didn't want her anymore. She knew what manner of good man Mo was. But they figured they knew better. After Mo's wife died, a large social worker with flat, runover shoes took her out of his home anyway.

At the time there was a county-wide decree that said orphans should be placed with relatives as a first result and foster care placement should be the absolute last result. They even agreed to pay the families to take their own relatives in. And that was how it all came together. When Mo Riley's wife died, the county searched under every rock for relatives, no matter how despicable those relatives were, and out of the woodwork came the Henleys. Ma Henley was a distant cousin of Janet's deceased mother and she and her family, for that money the county was willing to give them, would be more than happy to take her in.

Now, twelve years later, Janet was eighteen and of legal age in the eyes of the law and was getting out when they needed her to stay. When, the way Janet saw it, they needed that monthly check to keep-a-coming.

"It's a cruel and harsh world out there," Pa Henley said. "You don't know what you're about to get yourself into, little girl. It's cold outside."

Janet looked at him. He was the head of the family, who always sat at the head of the table, but Ma Henley wore the pants. When Janet first came to the family and was treated like their slave rather than their relative, she remembered looking to the kindly-faced man to help her. He reminded her of Mo Riley, whom she was missing something fierce. But that help never came. Pa Henley was better than the rest of those Henleys. He would be the one to tell them when enough was enough. But he was terrible too.

Since she was six years old, she'd been with them. Since she was six years old, she'd been the outcast. The one that was forced to wash the dishes and do the laundry and sweep the floors and take out the trash and clean up the throw-up when one of the Henley children got sick. Those children were bigger than her. Boy Henley was older than her. But she had to do their cleaning too.

And it wasn't up for discussion. Ma Henley would slap the fire out of her if she didn't do her cleaning right, and they'd let Boy Henley kick her for no other reason than the fact that he liked kicking things. She'd kick him back every time he kicked her, but that didn't sit well with either of the Henley parents. He'd run crying to them accusing her of abusing him and, for some inexplicable reason Janet could never understand, they believed him. They always believed that lying boy! And not only would Janet feel the wrath of Ma Henley, but on more than a few of her *kick-backs* it was Pa Henley himself who'd grab her and throw her down in their rat-infested basement, one of the few basements in all of Cope County, as punishment for defending herself. He'd defend her when his family's mistreatment crossed way over the line, but nobody touched his boy and girl, he'd tell her.

And now they all were telling her to stay.

"What you need to do," Boy Henley had the nerve to say, "is keep your scrawny butt right where you at. You'd be lost in the real world. What you gon' do in that world outside? Why they'd eat you alive!"

That from the boy who liked kicking things so much that he killed the family dog, just by kicking him to death. But all he had to do was say Jane did it. She said she didn't. No way would she harm that sweet dog. She was the only one crushed when he died. But Ma and Pa Henley believed their fat-faced bully boy the way they always did, and down in the basement Janet went. It started the first week of her arrival at their home and never let up, not ever, during the whole of her twelve years a slave.

From the moment she stepped foot into the Henley household they called her PJ, for Plain Jane, as Boy Henley mockingly informed her. "A face like a shovel, you've got," was how he loved to describe her. "And with a laugh like a hyena."

His mother was even more blunt. "You should be beautiful with your big hazel eyes most women would kill to have," she'd say. "But all together it just don't work for you." And they called her many names to describe her features. Horse-face. Shit-face. Crack-Baby-face. Or they'd just call her Jane. But her name was Janet.

When tomorrow came, and she left those Henleys once and for all, she was determined to reclaim her name.

"It's a cruel and harsh world you're about to step out into," Ma Henley said, joining in the chorus of the *devil you know is better than the devil you don't* torch song too. And it was true that Janet knew how bad they were. She held no illusions about the fact that the Henleys were truly the devil she knew. But that unforgiving world outside, in their view, was worse.

"Ain't no soft bed waiting for you," Ma Henley continued. "Not here in Cope County it ain't! Now you know that, Jane, don't you?"

"Yes, ma'am, I know it." They banged it into her head for years, as if they never wanted her servitude to end even back then. She had no choice but to know it. Problem was, she didn't believe it.

When she first came to live with them, she would try her little backtalk and try to be sassy with her tongue. Mo Riley didn't mind her speaking up for herself, and she had grown accustomed to talking back. But the first time she talked back in the Henley household, Ma Henley picked up that cast-iron rod and slammed it against her back, a hit so violent that it took her breath away and almost rendered her unconscious.

She learned a lesson that day.

She learned that those Henleys weren't playing. She learned that she was smart enough to get herself into survival mode, and to stay in survival mode if she expected to get out of there alive. Her tongue lost its sassiness almost immediately after that cast-iron rod hit to the back, and it became completely compliant. Now, all those years later, it was like an echo chamber. Whatever they said was right. Whatever they did was right. She wasn't rocking any boats. She wasn't stirring any pots. That was her fate and she was determined to live through it, and get to the other side.

"People out of work out there," Ma Henley continued to try and persuade her as they all sat around that dining room table having their last supper together. "People losing their homes and the shirts off their backs. It's worse than the Great Depression ever was. And you going out to that? You're just gonna be another poor black gal on the streets. Probably gonna have to do some horrible things with that body of yours just to get by. That's what's gonna befall you, child. It's a cruel and harsh world you're about to go out in."

Janet kept eating slowly as she listened to all of their big talk. She nodded as if she agreed with every word they spoke and was extra careful to look at whomever was talking at the time. She learned that when she was six years old after that rod hit. Pretend they were the wisest people in the world with wisdom just dripping from their salty tongues and, if she did it just right, no hit or kick or slap or basement punishment would come her way. And most times it worked. But sometimes even that wasn't enough.

And although she looked stone-faced as Ma Henley and the rest of the Henleys kept going on and on about that cruel and harsh world outside, she was so excited to be finally getting out of that prison that the idea of a cruel and harsh world sounded good to her!

Because she knew exactly why they were doing it. And it wasn't about any affection or concern they held for her. It was all about the Benjamins. It was all about their lifestyle. If Janet left, those first-of-the-month county checks would be gone too. If Janet left, who was going to do all that cleaning for such filthy folks? Who was going to take out the trash?

Boy Henley and Pa Henley were so lazy sometimes that both of them together wouldn't make half a man. If Janet left, who was going to give Boy Henley a target to kick during those times when he'd get so enraged that his face would look contorted and he'd put a hole in the wall?

She remembered many times when the whole family would be in Walmart and he'd be screaming like a madman across the aisles just because a salesperson didn't hurry over fast enough to tell him how much that video game cost. And then Ma Henley would start screaming at the salespeople, too, for not assisting her boy and start accusing them of running away rather than hurrying over to help their customers. And then the manager would rush over and make the whole family, including little Janet, leave.

But Boy Henley always got the last laugh. Before he left, he would take the whole bin of video games and knock it to the floor. Just tumble it over. That was how he was. And he'd be embarrassed when people looked at him like he was crazy with no home training, and then he'd go home and give Janet a black eye, taking his embarrassment out on her. And the Henleys, embarrassed by that whole shopping fiasco, too, would naturally blame Janet. "You saw how those white folks looked at us," they'd say. And they said it as if those white folks were looking at them because of Janet, not because of their own insane behavior.

But Ma Henley was sitting at that dining room table talking as if all those twelve years of torture never happened. As if they never treated her as if a dirty rag held more promise. And they expected her to believe the world outside was the problem?

"Why don't you stay here a little longer," Ma Henley kept talking, feeding her fat face and her own delusions. "Just because you're turning eighteen tomorrow doesn't mean you have to leave at exactly that time. The county will keep paying for you to stay with us until you're twenty-one, on account of you were an orphan, so I don't see what's all the rush. We're your family, Jane. We're the only family you got."

Family? The way they treated her? She'd admit she didn't know what it was like to be in a good family long term. She was placed in her first foster home when she was born. She moved from foster home to foster home and then, at the ripe old age of four, landed in a good one. But two years later, the old lady died. And they wouldn't let the widower Mo Riley take care of her even though he was more than capable of doing so. So she ended up with the Henleys.

And if family were people like them, she wanted no parts of *family*.

And that was why Janet kept on eating and listening. But never giving any opinion either way. She'd never been disrespectful to Ma Henley or Pa Henley in all the time she'd been in their house. Not because they deserved respect: they didn't. But because the Good Book said it was wrong to disrespect your elders and Janet tried to live her life the right way. Even though it was a hard life to live. Even though many nights she cried herself to sleep wondering if trying to live right was even worth it. Wondering if she should just kill'em all and be done with it.

But she held on. She was terrified of the world outside. They made sure she'd grow up terrified of that world. But compared to life with the Henleys, she was convinced the world outside would be a piece of cake.

And they wanted her to stay? They actually believed she would stay? Janet was looking at them as she sat at that dining room table, listening respectfully to them, but what they didn't realize was that she'd rather eat a skunk than stay with them.

"I hate to say this to you, Jane," Ma Henley finally said, "and you know it's coming from a place of love."

Janet looked her big hazel eyes at Ma Henley and waited for her to say it. It was what the Henleys always reverted to whenever they wanted to really twist the knife.

"You're a good girl," Ma Henley said. "You always have been. But you're so plain and ordinary-looking that beige is popping with color compared to you. And here in Cope County, no boy is gonna want somebody with your limited resources in the beauty department. Let's just be honest. Not when they can have their pick of the litter. Women outnumber men five to one in this town. What man's gonna choose you? And what in the world is a girl like you gonna do without a man?"

Live. Work. Take care of my own self. Be free!

Janet wanted to say all those things to Ma Henley. They were just bubbling inside of her waiting to be released. But that wasn't for anybody else to know. She didn't say a mumbling word. She just kept on eating.

And Ma Henley kept on begging. She wouldn't call it that. But Janet would. "The county only giving people like you that one-time payment of five hundred dollars when they turn eighteen and leave placement. That ain't enough money to even get an apartment. How you gonna live? You'll be homeless inside a week!"

What Janet may have lacked in the beauty department, she more than adequately made up in the brains department. She already was set up with a room in a boarding house that rented for fifty bucks a week. And she already had a job lined up, too, at a meat-packing plant that just hired a slew of workers. But she'd never tell the Henleys that.

Whenever Daughter Henley wasn't at home, Janet would get on her computer, go to the password-protected account she had secretly created, and apply for jobs. One job interviewed her over Skype. It was a minimum wage job at that meat-packing plant in Cope, but when she got the email saying she was among the batch of applicants hired, it was as if she'd won the lottery. It felt that good.

And then the day arrived. Janet's eighteenth birthday. Although the Henleys never let her go to school long enough to get a regular diploma like their children got, they did let her get her GED. And on that morning, on her birthday, she packed that GED and everything else she owned in the world, which was very little, and headed for the off ramp.

It should have been touching to her that the whole Henley family were all standing in the living room to see her off. After twelve years with those people? It should have been real touching.

But it wasn't touching at all.

It was liberating.

And they kept on begging. They kept going on and on about that harsh and cruel world she was about to embark upon, and she just held her fully packed beat-up suitcase as tightly as she could and let them beg. They were the harsh and cruel world to Janet. They were the bogeyman! And on that empowering morning, when she was finally an adult in the eyes of the law and could live on her own terms, she was not about to play the hypocrite. She was not about to smile in anybody's face when they'd spent twelve years spitting in hers.

"Remember we're your family," Pa Henley had the nerve to say, bitterness in his eyes as if she was abandoning them. "You'll need us before we need you!"

"Let her go," Boy Henley said. "I'm sure her scrawny butt will be back when that world outside shows her what it's made of. When that outside world overwhelms her dumb butt."

Janet wanted to set him straight right then and there. She wanted to tell Boy Henley that *they* overwhelmed her, what was he talking about? That they showed her, day in and day out, what they were made of! How could that world outside be any worse than them?

But she didn't say a word. Mo Riley always told her to never burn bridges. When he told her that, she was a little kid and didn't know what he meant. "Who burns bridges?" she asked him. But he was clear. Be able to walk back across that bridge if you have to, he told her, and walk back across with your head held high.

That was why she didn't cuss out the Henleys. That was why she didn't stoop to their level and gave them a piece of her mind the way she'd been wanting to do for years on end. She kept her mind intact, kept her head held high, and walked on across that bridge.

To the other side.

CHAPTER TWO

In that world outside the bus put her out miles away from the Henley house, at the end of a busy block on Grundy Street, and she suddenly felt naked and alone. She was truly all by herself now. After twelve years a slave, it would take some getting used to.

She held her suitcase against her small frame and nervously looked at her paper that contained the address of the boarding home that was about to become her new home. And then she began heading in that direction.

What surprised her about that world outside was how different it felt. How busy it was. How there were so many people just milling about and going about their daily lives with laughter and talk as if they had nothing but time on their hands. And Janet smiled too. Because she felt free. Because it reminded her of where she lived when she lived with Mo Riley and his sweet wife. But Boy Henley was right about one thing. It did feel overwhelming!

And to get to her new home, she first had

to walk by a group of men standing near the corner, up to no good, and laughing at her. Or trying to hit on her. She didn't know which.

"Hey, you," one of them said to her. But Janet knew enough to know to keep on walking.

"He's talking to you, gal," said another one. "Why you won't answer the man? And you know you hear us!"

"Just look at yourself," said a third one. "Looking all colonial in your *Little House on the Prairie* dress!"

And they all laughed again when he said that.

Janet knew why they were laughing. She wore a long dress with a sash in the back just like those children from the *Little House on the Prairie* tv show used to wear. But that was all the Henleys bought her. Dresses like that. But she'd already planned to use a few of the five hundred dollars the State gave to her when she left placement, and buy herself some clothes. Just a few outfits to get started. And long dresses with sashes in the back were not on her list. They could laugh all they wanted. One day, with God's help, she was gonna laugh too.

And she kept on walking.

But when she got to that boarding house at the other end of the block, her heart sank. It was a rundown rathole. There was no other way to describe it. And when the landlady walked her up the stairs to the room she was about to rent for fifty bucks a week, that room, too, was a rundown, filthy rathole in a boarding house filled with rundown, filthy people. Online it was the cheapest room she could find that looked halfway decent. That looked like a place she could lay her head.

But in reality, as she paid the lady and the lady gave her the keys, and as she walked back up those rickety stairs and unlocked the door, she realized that those photos online were fake. She knew for certain when she sat on the lumpy bed, and a rat the size of a cat ran out from beneath it as if he was affronted that she had disturbed him, and he darted out in search of a better hiding place.

But Janet Evans had spent many nights in a rat-infested basement at the Henleys. In so-called punishment. It would take more than a big rat to disturb her peace.

But it did give her some pause as she sat on that bed with her suitcase on her lap and looked out through a dusty old window. It did make her wonder if her whole life was going to be one big punishment after another one, just like the Henleys said it would be. As if she deserved it. As if she had spent her entire existence committing unforgiveable crimes when she'd, to her knowledge, had never committed any crimes at all!

But she wasn't going to dwell on it. She had a job, and she had a plan. She would save, and in a few years, if she played her cards right, she was going to have her own apartment. And it was going to be clean and nice and in a good area. And in a few years after that, she was going to be buying her very own home. That was her plan. And no cat-sized rat, or lumpy old bed would ever be enough to derail her.

She sat her suitcase down and got to cleaning her room as best she could. It was what it was, but she was going to make the best of it. And she unpacked her suitcase. She still had that transistor radio Pa Henley had given her one day, and she turned it on. She didn't know who was singing, and she barely understood the words because the reception was so poor, but at least it was company for her.

The first time she saw Richard would be four years later, during orientation at the brand-new Shetfield textile mill in Cope, a job she secured after the meat-packing plant she worked for was permanently shut down by government regulators. It was her first day on her new job. And by the end of that day, she would not believe her good fortune.

CHAPTER THREE

FOUR YEARS LATER

An empty garage in a building Richard Shetfield owned, and Myron Colby, his head accountant, was still going down the list. It started with petty thefts, easy to overlook small-dollar amounts, but then the amounts began getting larger and larger. "And on October third," Myron said, "he took a whopping fifty thousand dollars, Boss."

Myron was sitting down. So was Pourtnoy, the thief and an accountant in one of Richard's branch offices. He sat in the middle of the room. And Richard was pacing the floor. A few steps forward and then he'd turn around and pace those same steps again. All in front of Pourtnoy's chair. All in his fancy suit and his fancy shoes. All with a metal crowbar in his hand. "Fifty thousand dollars," Richard said as he walked and turned, trying with all he had to contain his rage. "Fifty thousand dollars!"

"On October seventh, just four days later," Myron added, "he took an additional fifty thousand, Boss."

Richard shook his head. "Another fifty. A hundred grand in four days. *Got*damn," Richard said as his face contorted into an angry scowl. And then he stopped pacing, held that crowbar up as if it were a baseball bat, and slammed it into Pourtnoy's legs.

Pourtnoy cried out in horror, grabbing his legs.

"Keep going," Richard said to Myron, ignoring Pourtnoy's cries. "Go down the list. Tell me everything!"

"He took more like petty cash for a few weeks, but almost daily though. And then on November fifteenth," Myron said, "he took . . ." Myron frowned as he looked at the list closer, to make sure he was seeing it right. "He took . . ." And then he looked at Richard. "On November fifteenth," Myron said, amazement in his eyes, "he took two million dollars, Boss."

Richard already knew the amount. His investigators had already told him the amount. But just hearing it again did something to him. It was jarring to hear. He stopped pacing right in front of Pourtnoy's chair.

And Pourtnoy panicked. "I was going to give it back, Mr. Shetfield," he pleaded. "I wouldn't cheat you, Boss. You know that!"

"Two million dollars," Richard said as he

stared at Pourtnoy with disappointment and disgust in his eyes. "You cooked my books to the tune of two million dollars."

"I took it," Pourtnoy admitted. "But I was going to give it right back. I swear to you I was!"

"Was that your money to take?" Richard asked him.

"I was going to give it back, sir," Pourtnoy pleaded again.

"Was that your money, I said? Or was it my money?"

"It was yours. You know it was yours."

"But you took it anyway?"

"I was going to give it back."

"But you took it anyway!" Richard yelled out with such venom that even Myron jumped.

"Yes sir!" Pourtnoy admitted. "I took it anyway."

Richard settled back down. "That's some serious disrespect, Pourtnoy. Wouldn't you say so, Myron? Wouldn't you call that serious disrespect?"

"I most certainly would, Boss," said Myron, and then he looked at Pourtnoy too. "Serious disrespect."

"That's what I call it," Richard said, and then he threw that crowbar aside.

Pourtnoy watched as the crowbar clanged against the concrete flooring and then rolled against the wall.

When he looked back at Richard, Richard had picked up a long, rusty nail that laid on the bare floor. And before Pourtnoy could even flinch, Richard took that nail and angrily stabbed it all the way through Pourtnoy's left eye.

Pourtnoy fell over his chair screaming in agony, and even Myron jumped up from his own chair in disbelief. He looked as Pourtnoy twisted around on that floor in unbearable pain, with blood gushing out, and then he looked at Richard. He'd heard about those Shetfields and what happened to people when they crossed them, but he'd never seen it up close and personal before. It stunned him.

"Call the squad," Richard said, trying to regain his composure. "Tell them to get over here, clean up the place, and drop him off at the hospital. And I mean drop."

"Yes, sir," said Myron.

But then Richard, still angry, ran up to Pourtnoy and leaned down to him, screaming at him. "That's what happens to motherfuckers who steal from me! That's what happens! That's what happens! Do you understand me now?!"

"Yes, sir!" Pourtnoy cried. "Yes, sir, I understand you. Yes, sir!"

"Don't fuck with me. Don't you ever fuck

with me!"

"No, sir. Never, Mr. Shetfield. No, sir!"

Richard was breathing heavily. He continued to stare at his accountant. He continued to fight against that rage he felt. And then he stood erect again. "You're going to put every dime of that money back into my account."

Pourtnoy was nodding. "Yes, sir. Right away, sir."

"When?"

"Right away, sir. Right away!"

Then Richard calmed back down. "When the hospital releases you," he said to his accountant, "put the money back into my account. You have forty-eight hours to get it done. Then I expect to see you back on the job Monday morning. Understood?"

Pourtnoy looked his one good eye at his boss, as the blood continued to gush out of his inverted eye. Back on the job? Was this man for real? But he didn't question it. He nodded his head. "Yes, sir," he said.

And then Richard began walking toward the exit. Myron, still shocked, looked at Pourtnoy, and then hurried behind Richard. "But Boss," he said.

Richard turned slightly, but kept on walking. "Yes?"

Myron tried to keep pace with him. "Is it

wise to keep him in your employ, sir?"

"Very wise."

"But he stole from you."

"He's going to return the money."

"Yes, sir, I heard that. But the fact remains, sir," Myron said when they arrived at the exit door and they both stopped walking, "he stole from you."

"One thing for certain," said Richard, "is that he stole from me. Another thing for certain? He'll be my best accountant ever. You know why?"

"Why, sir?"

"Look at him. That's why. He's one fucking eyeball short of a pair! He'll never steal from me again. I guarantee you that," Richard said, pulled open the door, and left.

Myron ran his hands through his hair. He knew working for the Shetfields would pose challenges, but he never envisioned this kind of challenge. Because he could only imagine what would happen to him if he crossed them too!

Then he heard Pourtnoy's screams for help again, remembered what Richard had ordered him to do, and he quickly pulled out his cell phone.

CHAPTER FOUR

It was Janet's first day at the textile mill, sitting in an auditorium filled with the other new hires, when she needed to tip out to go use the restroom. She'd heard rumors that the big man was onsite, but she had no idea she'd ever run into him. But that was exactly what she had done. She literally ran into him!

She was rounding the corner, heading for the restroom stalls, and he was turning the corner, heading away from the restroom stalls. They collided.

For him, it felt like running into a marshmallow.

For her, it felt like running into a brick wall. She was knocked backwards and fell on her rear.

"Oh, my!" he said, reaching for her, but her rear had hit the floor before their hands connected.

And when their hands did connect, Janet felt an electric current zip through her body as if it was an occupying force. Wondering why, she looked up into his eyes. Who was this?

She had no idea it was Richard Shetfield she was staring at. She had no idea it was the very namesake of the factory she now worked for that had knocked her down.

She had no idea that that one brief encounter would set the standard for her for the rest of her life.

Because she looked into his eyes. His stark, bright green eyes. And saw nothing but kindness there.

"Are you injured?" he asked as he took her, not just by the hand, but by the elbow, too, and helped her to her feet. She was twenty-two years old by then, but always looked small for her age. But one thing was for certain to Janet, just looking at his muscular body: he wasn't small for *his* age!

"I'm not injured at all," she said, standing up. "My pride a little," she admitted, dusting her skirt off, "but not me."

He smiled. "Well there's that," he said. But when she suddenly looked up at him as she continued to dust herself off, as if she didn't get what he meant by *there's that*, a jolt of something electrifying shot through Richard's body as if her eyes had pierced him, shocking the shit out of him. *What the hell was that*, he wondered. And he began staring at her as if he were studying her.

But for Janet, it was nothing more than an awkward moment of silence where she found herself staring at him in such a gawking way that he couldn't bring himself to just walk on by. Especially since he'd knocked her down.

But that wasn't why Richard didn't just leave. He had been jolted into staying. It was as if he was being ordered to pay attention to this one. Don't just walk away from her. Pay attention to her! But why? To say she wasn't his type would be an understatement. She had an interesting face. He'd admit she had a somewhat unique face in that it bore a strength and sophistication that a woman that young shouldn't possess. But what did that have to do with him?

He extended his hand. "I'm Richard Shetfield," he said. Saying his name alone had always been his trump card whenever he wanted to impress a woman. Everybody in those parts knew that name and reacted accordingly. Not that he wanted to impress this particular woman, he told himself. Why would he?

But Janet responded differently than all those other women before her had. She seemed more shocked than impressed.

And he was right. Janet was completely shocked. She had just literally run into THE

Richard Shetfield, the very namesake of the company she now worked for! And immediately she went into survival mode. Would he fire her for bumping into him like a crazy woman? She'd always heard the Shetfields were just awful people. They owned most of Oklahoma, she'd been told, and never treated their workers right. Was all that talk wrong?

She shook his hand, forgetting to introduce herself.

But he needed to know her name. Maybe he knew her. Maybe that was why he was so intrigued with her. "And you are?" he asked her.

His hair was like a light-brown pile of silk that made his eyes look even starker, Janet thought. And when he ran his hand through that hair, it came back in a pile across his forehead. He really was a very handsome man. He really was so out of her league that she had no business to even pretend to be on the same playing field.

And for some reason, that jolt of reality gave her more confidence. Forget dreaming, she told herself. Get on with keeping your job, and living your own life. A life, she knew even then, that could not possibly involve that impossibly handsome man. "I'm Janet," she said with a smile, giving more grip to her handshake. "I'm Janet Evans."

Her sudden aliveness seemed to relax him far more than her gawking did. As if he was accustomed to the gawking of females but didn't care for that kind of attention.

"Nice to meet you, Miss Evans," he said, and then leaned against the wall and folded his arms. He couldn't stop staring at her. He didn't understand why he was even interested. She had nice hazel eyes and a strong constitution about her, but it wasn't as if she was some exotic beauty he couldn't wait to ravage. Far from it. But he also knew what he was experiencing wasn't so much as physical as it was emotional. It was some kind of an odd, strange, emotional reaction to her. As if he knew her. As if she was somebody near and dear to him when he was reasonably certain he'd never laid eyes on her before.

But he was seeing something within her that captivated him. And to call it a physical attraction would demean what he was seeing. Because he'd never felt that way before.

But he couldn't figure out why he felt that way. Had he eyed her from afar, he would not have been impressed at all. She would have been just another ordinary face in a crowd of ordinary faces. But up close and personal, and looking her in her eyes, and just being next to her made him realize there was nothing ordinary about her. Nothing!

But he still couldn't put his finger on why he felt that way!

Janet didn't notice his feelings, but she noticed how he not only folded his big arms, but he crossed his legs at the ankle, too, as if he was getting comfortable around her. "You're one of the new hires, I imagine," he said to her.

He was much older than her. Maybe as much as ten years older, if she had to guess. "Yes, sir, I am," she said.

"What do you think of the place?"

"Oh, I think it's wonderful," she said excitedly. Then, after saying it, she scrunched-up her face.

Richard almost smiled. She looked constipated. "What's that look about?" he asked her.

"Truth is," Janet said, "if I were you, I wouldn't take my word for it."

What a curious thing to say, he thought. "Why not?" he asked her.

"Because I'm not a good judge of whether it's a wonderful place or not," she said. "After losing my job at the meat plant, I'm happy to have a job. I would have thought a sewer was lovely had it hired me too."

Richard laughed out loud. Who was this

girl, he wondered! "Very true," he said.

Then he glanced down at her breasts, which, for her small frame, were quite sizeable. But why would he be glancing down there, Janet wondered. It was impossible that there was any attraction!

But he glanced down there again. Which now rendered her even more uncomfortable than she had been when she first laid eyes on him. Time to go, she decided.

"I'd better get going," she said, "before I'm late getting back to orientation."

"Of course," he said, standing erect. And if she didn't know better, he seemed almost embarrassed by his roaming eyes. "Off you go," he added like the rich people talked to people like her, and she left his side.

But as she walked away, she glanced back at him. To her surprise, he was glancing back at her, too, and she could see his eyes roam down to her butt. Which made her blush with heat, and she quickly looked away.

"Are you okay, sir?" It was Lance Colvin, the line supervisor. He was walking up just as Richard had given Janet a second look.

He wanted to ask more about her. He'd never in his life been captivated by a woman he'd just laid eyes on before. Not ever!

But he didn't go there. Leave the poor

child alone, he decided. He wouldn't even love her and leave her. He'd just leave her. Like every woman he'd ever been with, he would mean her no good. "I'm okay," he said, and walked away.

But their little encounter put a smile on Janet's face that would last the whole day. She was no dreamer, she thought, as she made her way to the restroom. She knew he couldn't possibly be attracted to her. How could he be attracted to a shit face? To horse face? To Plain Jane?

But he wasn't repulsed, either, the way the Henleys declared every man would be.

She even looked in the mirror when she got in the restroom, something she rarely ever did. And suddenly she liked what she saw. It wasn't beauty. Her face was too long and her eyes were too large and her mouth was too small to be classified that way. Her face was too asymmetrical to be thought beautiful. But her brown skin was smooth as silk. And her high cheekbones gave her an elegant look. And her ears and nose were at least proportionate to her face. She liked what she saw because she saw confidence. She saw a young woman trying to make it on a new job, still trying to make it in that world outside, and it all held such possibilities.

Was it her confidence that he saw, too, that made him give her that second look? Or was it just her boobs? Because those, she knew, were also positive attributes of hers, she thought with a playful grin.

Then she suddenly realized the time, hurried into the stall to pee, and then washed her hands quickly, grabbed a paper towel, and ran back to orientation.

CHAPTER FIVE

Richard's sportscar sped away from the textile mill and turned onto a long country road that was the main road to downtown Cope, and to get out of town. Unlike Tulsa, where he was headed and that was less than a half-hour away, it was quiet at night in Cope. But not so quiet in his car. Because one of his lady friends had him on the phone, and she was getting on his last nerve.

"I told you I wouldn't have time," he said into his car phone.

"Why not, Dicky? It's not as if I ever ask you for anything."

"Damn right you don't ask me for anything. We're just friends, remember? Friends with benefits."

"The only person this relationship is benefitting is you!"

Richard grinned. "I'm sure it's got perks for your ass, too," he said as he noticed a young woman walking on the side of the road. Her skirt was short, revealing very nice legs, and her hair was nicely done, too, he noticed, in curls just pass her neckline. It was not unusual to see country girls walking down those country roads

PLAIN JANE EVANS AND THE BILLIONAIRE

at night, as if their backward asses had no clue how dangerous it was. They wouldn't pull that shit in Tulsa, he thought, and drove right by her.

But as he drove passed her and was able to look through his rearview mirror and get a glimpse of her face from the illumination of the streetlight, he suddenly realized who she was. The girl that had intrigued him that morning. And he frowned. "What the. . ." he found himself saying, as he slammed on brakes.

"What did you just say?" his lady friend asked him over the phone. "I was asking you what perks are you talking about, and you said *what the* something. What did you just say?"

"I'll talk to you later," Richard said, threw his phone on the hook, and began backing up his Porsche toward the young lady.

He pressed down his passenger side window and leaned over. "Hey, you," he said. He had to keep driving to keep up with her fast walking.

But Janet kept walking because he sounded just like those men on her street with the *hey you* line. She ignored him. She had pepper stray on her, too, if it came to that.

But Richard was shocked. She was ignoring *him*? Didn't that beat all? Although, he also realized, it was nighttime on a country road and he was virtually a stranger to her. It was the right thing for her to do.

Then he suddenly remembered her name. "Janet!" he yelled out to her.

It was only when she heard her name did she bother to look his way. And that was when she saw who was behind the wheel. And her heart soared when she saw who it was. At least she wouldn't have to soak him down and use up her can of pepper stray, she figured. "Mr. Shetfield," she said with a big smile on her face, and walked up to his car window.

But Richard was oddly upset. "What are you doing out here this time of night?"

"I'm on my way home."

"But why are you walking? Don't you have a car?"

Janet barely had a roof over her head. "No, sir," she said. "And the bus left before orientation turned out. There was another one coming in another hour, but I figured if I walked, I'd be home by then."

Richard understood she'd be anxious to get home after a long day at work. But her ass should have realized the danger too. "Get in," he said.

Janet was surprised that he would invite somebody like her to ride in his fancy car, but she wasn't the kind of person who questioned goodness. It was too far and in between in her life to ever question goodness. Especially coming from a man who owned the company she worked for. Especially coming from a man with such kind eyes. She got into his car.

"I don't normally get into a stranger's car," Janet said with a smile as she closed the door.

But Richard was still upset for some reason. "Then why did you get into mine?" he responded with no warmth whatsoever.

Janet looked at him. She was used to people talking to her that way, with no interest in how it made her feel. But she was disappointed when that kind of harshness came from him. She had thought of him, when she first met him, as one of the good guys. She wanted to say she could get back out, to repay harshness with harshness, but he owned the company she worked for. She didn't go there.

But when Richard saw that sudden sad look in her big eyes, he quickly realized his usual bluntness apparently came across as cruel to her. But for some unfathomable reason he was still upset that she was walking on that dark road alone at night. "I didn't mean to sound harsh," he said to her. "I apologize for that."

That was a first for Janet. Somebody actually admitting they spoke out of turn to her? She knew he was different than all the rest. She knew it! She saw it in his eyes the first time they met. "Thank you," she said to him.

"Buckle your seatbelt," he said, and she quickly did as he said.

He pulled off again, driving. "Where do you live?" he asked her.

"I live at the end of Grundy Street."

"At the end of what street?"

She smiled. "Grundy Street. It's just up the road a piece. It's near downtown."

"Never heard of Grundy Street," he said. "But I'm not exactly a Cope native, either," he added, as he drove.

She looked at him. "Where are you from?"

"Born and raised in Tulsa. But then my father decided to pack up the family and move us all to Texas. I came back and launched a few businesses across Oklahoma, and put down roots again in Tulsa. Which isn't far from here."

"Not far. But it's a world apart," said Janet. "I've gone there many times with my foster. . . people." She still refused to refer to the Henleys as her foster *family*. "It's big."

"Bigger than Cope, that's for sure," he said and glanced down at those nice legs he had noticed before. "I didn't recognize you from behind, or I would have stopped immediately."

Janet looked at him. "Why?" It wasn't as if he knew her like that.

Richard had to think about her question. "I don't rightly know," he said. Then he looked at her. "But I would have stopped."

She smiled. His eyes were so soft! "Thank you," she said.

Her eyes were beautiful to Richard, too, and looking into her eyes made him look down at her body. She was a small girl, but she had curves in all the right places. And a nice set of tits to round out the package. He could have a very good night rolling in the hay with her. Which, he knew, would be totally taking advantage of a sweet kid like her. But that was how he usually saw women: as objects of desire. As somebody to do it with. That was how he was raised. That was how he spent his life believing was the way it was done. Because in his circle, that was how it was done. And just looking at Janet's nice legs, and what he knew were between those nice legs, was making him horny.

But he needed to find out if she lived alone.

"I'm right you know," he said to her.

Janet looked at him as he drove. Did she miss a conversation? "You're right about what?"

"About Tulsa," said Richard. "It isn't far from here. Just a quick twenty-minute drive if that long." Then he looked at the darkness outside. "Or what does a guy have to do around here? Get a room?"

Janet smiled. "Rather than drive twenty miles?"

That wasn't what he meant, but he went with it. "If the guy is tired and doesn't want to drive twenty miles, sure. And who are you to talk? You didn't want to wait a mere hour for the bus."

Janet laughed. He had her there. "True," she said.

"Are there any good hotels around here? Or," he said as if it was a sudden idea, "maybe you could put me up."

Janet's heart dropped at the thought of a man like him coming to her modest room. It was clean. She kept her room spotless. But it was still in a rathole.

"Or would you make me drive all the way to Tulsa all sleepy, and I fall asleep at the wheel and end up dead in a ditch? Would you let that happen to me, Janet?"

Janet wouldn't. But he already knew that. "No, sir. And I have a couch you can sleep on, if that'll help."

Richard smiled. He still had it! "It'll help indeed," he said. Because he knew, if he was going to be sleeping on her couch, she was going to be sleeping with him. "But what about your family?" he added, just to be certain. "Would I be disturbing them?"

"Oh, not at all. I live alone," she said, and that was all he needed to hear.

And he drove them, on her directions, to the boarding house on Grundy Street.

But when he stopped at the curb and got out of his car, and he looked up and down the poverty-stricken street, and then at the dilapidated boarding house that she called home, he was stunned.

He didn't expect a palace. He didn't expect her to live lavishly or in any way above her means. And he knew he didn't exactly pay his workers great wages.

But *damn*, he thought.

CHAPTER SIX

Janet could see the shock all over his handsome face. And a part of her was ashamed. Being poor never felt like real poverty until you saw it through somebody else's eyes. And Richard had the kind of eyes that couldn't camouflage what he was seeing. He even opened his sports jacket and placed his hands on his hips, like he was just blown away by how poor she truly was. She was hoping he'd tell her never mind and get in his car and leave. To spare them both the humiliation. But he didn't. He followed her into the building and up the stairs to her room.

The smells of urine and liquor were rampant throughout their walk upstairs and Janet could have just died when she took it all in herself. She was used to the smells. Sometimes she didn't even smell it at all. But she smelled it acutely that night.

When they got up to the door, and she pulled out the key, she glanced back at Richard. He was looking down the hall at another tenant, an older man who had slid down the wall and was drinking liquor out of a brown paper bag and talking to himself. And a couple could be heard screaming at each other in another room, and Richard kept glancing at that room too.

But when he realized Janet was looking at him, he looked away from the drunk tenant and looked at her. He didn't try to smile it off or make light of it with some lame joke, as if that kind of poverty wasn't shocking. Even Janet knew it was. She appreciated that he didn't pretend it wasn't.

She unlocked her room door. And they went inside of her one-room flat where the couch and the bed and the small kitchenette with a two-seat table comprised the whole of her living space. The bathroom required a walk down the smelly hallway outside of her room, as did the shower stalls.

Although her room itself smelled nice inside, and everything was clean and in its proper place, the walls were still peeling paint, and the ceiling still had holes in it where she kept buckets nearby to capture rain, and her closet had a curtain hanging instead of a door. Richard, who hailed from the richest family in Oklahoma, had never seen such adject poverty in his life. And he didn't know what to make of it.

Janet saw his confusion, too, but didn't help him. This was her life and she wasn't going to make excuses for it. Considering her background, she was a success story. It might not look that way to him, but she knew she was.

She went to the sink to wash her hands. "Would you care for something to eat?" she asked him, glancing back at him.

"To eat?" His intention had been to be eating her right about now, which he now felt ashamed of. "No," he said. "I'm good. But you go right ahead."

"I intend to. I'm starved. I cooked a pot of spaghetti this morning before I left for work."

Richard smiled. "You cooked an entire pot of spaghetti before you went to work?"

"Yes, I did," she said, drying her hands. "I didn't want to have to do it after work."

"What time do you leave for work?"

"Orientation started at eleven. So I had time this morning. But my official work hours beginning tomorrow will be six to three. So I'll probably get up at four and leave by five, to get over there in time."

Richard didn't know what to say to that. Get up at four and leave by five? Was she serious? He couldn't recall a time he'd ever gotten out of bed at four in the morning. He'd gone to bed at that time many times before, if he was out partying or otherwise doing whatever with some female. He couldn't even comprehend such an early rise.

"That's the couch," she said to him, which brought him back out of his musings. "Or would you prefer the bed?"

Richard looked at her. Was that some veil attempt at inviting him to her bed? He hoped so! "The bed?" he asked her.

"Sure," Janet said. "I don't mind sleeping on the couch if you'll be more comfortable in the bed."

Richard smiled again. Was this girl for real? Or was she just pulling his leg with that sweet lil' ol' me bullshit?

He decided to find out.

He removed his sportscoat and tossed it on the couch. "Come here for a second," he said to her.

Janet, who was just opening the refrigerator, found his request odd. She looked at him. He had removed his coat, revealing what even she could see was a very well-built body. She closed the door of the frig and walked over to him. "Yes?"

He placed both hands on her shoulders. He looked her dead in the eyes. "I'm very pleased to have an industrious young woman like yourself working at my mill," he said to her.

Janet smiled. She wasn't used to compliments. "Thank you, Mr. Shetfield. Thank you very much."

"Oh, let's dispense with the *Mister* crap. Richard is fine. But never Mister Shetfield."

Janet smiled. "Okay. Richard." She already liked that name. "Thank you."

"Don't mention it," Richard said, pulling her into his arms. He knew he'd get a hard-on holding her, and he was right. His penis began to have an erection as soon as his hands felt her soft back and his penis felt her soft body. He pulled her closer, so that she could feel him too.

But Janet was too busy feeling the simplest fact that a man was holding her. She'd never been held, in that way, by any man before in her entire life. Her entire body felt flushed with heat as Richard held her.

And he was feeling the heat too. She really did turn him on! And he moved one of his muscular thighs between her slender legs, to make certain she felt his erection. But when he did it, he suddenly could feel her heartbeat quicken to such an extent that it was alarming even to him. And then he could hear her heart pound.

Concerned, he pulled back from her. Was she alright?

She wasn't. He saw that right away. Her smooth skin was now flushed with anxiety, as if she'd never felt a man's penis before in her life, and he could see that it had terrified her.

54

And it was at that very moment did he realize what he had seen in her when he first laid eyes on her. It wasn't her body. It wasn't her big boobs. It was her innocence! That was what he saw. A truly sweet, kind, innocent young woman with truly sweet, kind, innocent intentions. No hidden agendas. No slickness and slyness like he had come to expect from females. And his bad ass was about to take advantage of a person like that? He was about to steal her virginity as if he were stealing candy? Because it would definitely be a theft coming from a man of his lifelong experience. It would be like the bad man taking candy from the sweet child. He knew he could do it. He knew how to talk his way into any woman's bed. But he also knew he couldn't do that to her. Not to this girl.

Mostly because he remembered that warning. Pay attention to this one. Pay attention to her!

He wasn't used to paying attention to women. Especially when he wanted what he wanted from that particular woman. And her innocence threw him for a loop. Every woman in his circle lost their virginity before they were sixteen years old. And he should know since most of them lost it to him! It was just how it was done in his world and he assumed it was done that way everywhere else too. And perhaps it was. But not with this one.

"You know what?" he asked her.

"What?" Janet responded, still trying to come back down from that place where the press of his penis and where him having his arms around her had taken her to.

"I wouldn't mind a little of that spaghetti myself," he said. "Is you can spare some."

And just like that, Janet came back down to earth. And she smiled that beautiful white smile that made him feel like an ass for taking her there. "I have plenty," she said to him. "I'll be happy to share." And she headed back to the refrigerator.

His goal was to eat with her, so that she wouldn't blame herself when he abruptly left. Because he was definitely leaving. No way was he spoiling this kid. No way. And he was going to make it his business to never see her again.

But as they sat at that tiny table together and ate what turned out to be a very good meal, he actually enjoyed himself. Even Janet could see he was having fun. He was the first human being to ever step foot in her room, after four years of renting that room, and she was pleased he was the first. Because there was something so decent about Richard. She couldn't say for certain why she felt that way, but that was what she saw in his eyes. And the eyes, as they say, were the window to the soul.

They sat at her little table in her little room and laughed and talked and ate good food together. And when he had finished, Richard found himself lingering, and talking some more. Mainly about her.

"When I first picked you up," he said, "you mentioned your foster people."

She remembered.

He smiled. "What's that?"

"I was in foster care all of my childhood," Janet said.

"Oh! You were talking about your foster *family*."

If you want to call them that. "Yes."

"So, I take it your family of origin wasn't around or?"

"No," said Janet. "There had been a car accident. My father died instantly, but my mother, pregnant at the time, was rushed to the hospital. She stayed alive long enough to give birth to me." She scrunched up her face. "But then she died too."

Richard was truly sorry. "Oh, I am so sorry, Janet."

"She stayed around long enough to make sure I was alright," Janet said. "I think that's what drives me. Knowing my mama made such a sacrifice for me to be here."

"She'll be proud of you," Richard said.

"I haven't done anything to be proud of," Janet said bluntly. "But at least I'm a good person. I think that'll probably count more with her."

Richard smiled. "That's absolutely true," he said. "And don't you ever forget that."

Janet smiled. "Want more?" she asked.

"You have more?" he asked.

"Plenty," she said. "I told you I cooked a whole pot full."

"Then yes," said Richard. "It's so good that my greedy ass will be pleased to go another round."

Janet laughed, stood up, and took his plate to refill it.

He was really enjoying her company. But he knew he wasn't helping her. The best thing a joker like him could ever do for her was to leave and leave expeditiously.

But she was so sweet, and so kind, and she actually laughed at his jokes. He didn't want to leave.

But he had to. She deserved a man who would stay and love her. He only knew how to leave, and what was love?

Before things got out of hand, and before she decided she could trust her heart with him when he knew she couldn't, he got up and headed for the couch to grab his sportscoat.

He glanced at his Rolex. It was almost eleven. "Damn, it's late."

"What time is it?"

"Eleven."

Janet was shocked. "That late?" She stood up too.

Richard smiled. "We were talking," he said.

"Yes, we were," Janet agreed with a smile of her own. But when she realized he had grabbed his coat, she frowned. "But you can't leave this time of night," she said.

"I can't?" Richard was looking at her as he put on his coat.

"No! You were already sleepy," she said. "I can't let you drive all the way to Tulsa and end up in a ditch."

He laughed. "I can manage," he said.

"You're going to sleep on the couch just as we agreed, and then get up in the morning and go home."

Richard stared at her. It would be so easy for him to take advantage of her. So easy! She wouldn't see a joker like him coming. "I'm fine, Janet, thank you. Your spaghetti and good conversation woke me right up!"

But Janet would have none of it.

"Nonsense," she said. "Food puts you to sleep, it doesn't wake you up. As soon as you get on that road, you'll be drowsy again." She walked over to her chest of drawers, opened the bottom one and pulled out a blanket, and then grabbed one of the two pillows off her bed.

"Here you are," she said, handing the pillow and blanket to Richard.

"I thought you said I could have the bed," he said jokingly.

Janet thought he was serious. "You can!" she said emphatically. "Please do!"

"I'm joking, Janet," he said with a grin.

Janet laughed. "Thanks for the laugher. You really are a very nice man," she said, and began heading toward the bed.

But Richard grabbed her by the arm and stopped her progression. She looked at him. And he was sincere this time. "No," he said to her, "I'm not."

Janet stared into his eyes. She couldn't understand why he would make a special point to say that to her. Somebody says you're a nice guy, and you make it your business to tell them you aren't? What was she to make of that?

Richard saw her confusion too. She was just talking off-the-cuff, he realized. She didn't mean it. Why was he making a big deal out of it? And he let go of her arm.

As she grabbed up her nightgown and her bathing supplies and also, he noticed, cleaning supplies, he removed his sportscoat again and sat down on the couch and began removing his shoes. When she went out of the room to go to the bathroom down the hall, he laid on the couch and placed the blanket over his lower body. This was insane, he felt. Why didn't he just take his ass on while she was gone, and do them both a favor?

Because he couldn't.

Because he wanted to stay.

Because he wanted to make certain she would be okay overnight, before he took his leave.

Although, he also knew, he was going to take his leave. Nothing would become of that night. Nothing *could* become of it. He found her innocent. He was determined to leave her that same way.

His only prayer was that she'd find a real good guy, not some fraud like him. But somebody who wouldn't use or abuse her, but would fully appreciate the diamond he had. But that man could never be him. All the wrong he'd done in his life could never be made right, no matter who was trying to make it right.

By the time she made it back into the room, freshly scrubbed and with her nightgown on, Richard, satisfied that she was back safe, closed his eyes. Within minutes, he was fast asleep.

CHAPTER SEVEN

He woke up to the sound of her cries.

Not loud cries, but very soft sobs that barely registered. At first, he thought he was hearing things. That was how soft they were. Then he didn't recognize where he was. Then, when it all came back to him and he realized he was at Janet's place, he knew he wasn't hearing things. He was hearing her!

He quickly leaned up and looked over at her bed. She was still asleep, but her head was turning from side to side, she kept murmuring *where are you, where are you*, over and over again, as if something was terrifying her. He quickly threw that blanket off his body and hurried over to her bed.

"Janet?" he said softly, trying to awaken her without rousing her. "Janet?"

But her contortions became even more desperate. *Where are you*, she kept asking. *Where are you?*!

He had no choice. He shook her. "Janet!" he said louder.

And it was enough. She opened her big, beautiful hazel eyes. When she saw him hovering over her, she jumped straight up.

"It's okay," he said quickly. "It's me. Richard."

When she realized who it was, and remembered that she did, indeed, have a man in her room, she laid back down. "What happened?" she asked him.

"You were having a bad dream, my dear."

"A dream?"

More like a nightmare, Richard knew, but he didn't want to alarm her any more than she already was. "Seems like," he said.

She looked worried. And leaned up on her elbows. "What was I saying?" she asked.

"You kept asking where are you," Richard said. Was she asking *him*, he wondered?

Janet thought about her dream. And she remembered it. "I was in a room," she said, "and my parents were with me. I've never seen them before in my life. Not even a picture. Nobody's never even had a photograph to show me of either one of my parents. But they were right there with me. Both of them. Don't tell me how I knew it was them. I just knew it was them. But they didn't stay long. I was talking. And in the middle of my conversation, they got up and walked out. And they left me in that strange room alone. And I was so scared."

Richard could feel the anguish as she spoke. He touched her arm. Why she touched him so, he'd never know.

"And I kept asking where are you, as if they were playing hide and seek with me and I just knew they were going to turn back up. But they never did. I kept trying to figure out where they had gone. But they never came back."

"It's okay," Richard said to her. "Lay back down." He helped her lay back down on her pillow.

But he could still see the pain in her eyes. And then tears appeared in her eyes. "They never came back," she said to him.

And that did something to Richard. He didn't know why, but he felt her pain to the core of his being. And he leaned down and placed his arms around her. She leaned up, and hugged him, sobbing. And then he moved her over, got in bed with her, placed the covers over both of them, and held her gently. She continued to hold him. They were side by side wrapped in each other's arms.

They stayed that way as Janet and then Richard fell asleep. They stayed that way when Richard woke up, made sure she was still asleep, and went back to sleep again.

The next morning, when Richard woke up, Janet's back was to him, he was spooning her, and her nightgown had twisted up near her waist. Which meant his penis was jutted against her bare butt. And it was already fully aroused. So aroused that he wanted to unzip his pants, pull it out, and put it all the way inside of her. He wanted to feel that tight virgin vagina for himself. But he couldn't do that to her.

He, instead, pulled down her gown, moved off his side, and laid on his back. Janet was still fast asleep, and he was glad that she was, but not being able to get that relief had killed any sleep he still might have felt.

And then, to make matters worse, her loud-ass alarm clock sounded, causing him to jump. But she woke up stretching.

He looked at the clock on her bedside. It was her get up time. It was four am.

She was about to get out of bed, but he pulled her back. "No need to get up this early," he said. "I'll take you to work today."

"No," she said firmly. "Thank you, but no. I need to get used to my routine." And she didn't give him a chance to argue the point. She got out of bed.

Richard watched as she got her supplies together and was about to head out into the hall.

"Where's the men's room?" Richard asked her.

"Down the hall. The last door before the back stairwell."

"And the ladies' room?" Richard asked.

Janet wondered why he wanted to know that. "It's across from the men's room."

Richard nodded. And Janet headed on out.

Richard laid there momentarily, and then got up too. After a trip to the men's room, he made it back into her room, fully dressed, and waited for her to return. He looked around, at the books she read, at the food in her frig and cupboards, at the clothes in her tiny closet. She didn't have much, but she had taste, he recognized. And he sat back on her little couch, yawned, and waited. Looked at his cell phone, which he had switched off before he went to bed. He had twelve messages in need of his attention. He switched it off again.

By the time Janet made it back into her room, he was dressed and ready to go. She was in her bathrobe. And she smiled. "You're up."

"Before the crack of dawn for the first time in my life!"

Janet laughed. "Hopefully you got enough sleep to drive safely," she said.

"Oh, yes," he said, as he walked over to her. "Thank you, Janet."

"For what? You were great company!"

Richard smiled too. "Why don't you let

me take you to work? It's still dark outside."

"Darkness never bothered me," Janet said. "Besides, I want to get used to my new routine. I need to make sure I'm leaving enough time to get to work without being late. I need to know if the bus runs a different route in the early morning, if it makes more stops. I need to get used to this, and the sooner I start the better."

Richard nodded. He understood. She couldn't rely on a joker like him, and even she knew that. Better he got out while she was ahead.

He placed both hands on her shoulders. And looked her in the eyes. "Take care of yourself," he said to her with all sincerity.

"You too," she said to him, as a sadness came over her. She didn't want him to leave! Then she was upset with herself for feeling so emotionally needy.

And Richard lingered. He didn't want to leave her either! And he wondered why. Why didn't he just go?

And then he began looking from her eyes to her mouth. That wonderful mouth. And he couldn't help it. He thought about how great her bare ass felt jutted against him while they were in bed together, and how he didn't get any relief then, and how he still had that need. And he decided to kiss her. But that was all he was going to do, he told himself. Just a simple kiss. He leaned into her, still holding her by the shoulders, and kissed her on the lips.

Only it wasn't a simple kiss the way he thought it would be. She tasted so good that it became much more than sweet. It became passionate. So much so that even Janet was feeling the heat. And soon he was kissing her harder and harder and his penis was growing larger and larger and she was in the throes of unbridled passion for the first time in her life. And he wrapped her into his arms.

Janet didn't want it to end. And Richard couldn't let it end. She tasted just the wonderful to him.

And it was overwhelming. He knew how to pull back. He knew how to cut this shit off. But he couldn't do it. He deprived himself all night, something he'd never done before in his life. Now it was serious. He had to have it!

As they continued kissing, Richard walked her to the bed. He laid her down, hurriedly opened her bathrobe, revealing her beautiful brown body, and then he began squeezing and kissing and sucking her breasts.

Janet was arching as he made love to her breasts. It felt exactly as she thought it would feel and her entire body was reacting to that feeling.

And when he moved down her body, between her legs, and he began sucking and kissing and licking her there, she just knew she was having an orgasm. It felt just that good.

But she wasn't there yet. She realized it when Richard stood up, removed his shoes, unbuckled his pants and pulled them, along with his briefs, all the way off. He pulled a condom out of his pocket before tossing his pants aside, put it on, and then laid on top of Janet, kissing her again. And then he entered her.

And as soon as she felt that thick meat push its way into her body, all of those good feelings she had been feeling made a sudden reversal, and turned into pain. Excruciating pain.

Richard knew he was against her hymen. He knew it was painful for her to allow him to push through. And although it felt good before he entered her, now that he was inside of her, those good feelings were in the stratosphere. Because she was so tight. Because she was so wet. And he kept moving, easing further and further in. And he couldn't stop. He looked at her, to see if she wanted him to stop. She was almost in tears because of the pain, and when he saw it, he stopped all movement. But Janet shook her head.

"I'm okay," she said, fighting back tears.

"Are you sure?"

"I'm positive," she said like the trooper he knew she was.

"It'll feel better," he said to her. "I promise you."

She tried to smile. "Okay," she said. She was committed now. There was no going back now. "Keep going."

And he kept going. He laid all the way down on top of her, wrapped her even tighter into his arms, and pushed on through. But he realized he had a problem. He hadn't felt such tightness in such a long time that it overtook his senses and he gave a fast push that bust through all of her resistances and took him to the other side. And then he began to bang.

But when he was on the other side, and was banging the crap out of her, the pain didn't get worse the way Janet thought it would. But it began to ease. And the more he made love to her, the more those good sensations returned, and she began to enjoy it once again. Richard was right! It did get better.

And that was when she experienced the first orgasm of her life. She thought she had climaxed when his mouth was between her legs, but she realized how wrong she was. Those feelings were nice. And sweet. But his oral was nothing like the real thing. She was arching and pulsating and barely able to bear it, when she came.

And her excitement and that tightness that still kept his dick throbbing, caused Richard to cum too. And he poured into that condom with so much cum, and with so much force, that it broke. And he felt it when it broke. He felt it when the cum that was in that condom began to pour out and into Janet.

And that broken condom was rolling down his penis, and he was feeling her rawness. Which only heightened his cum. So much so that he was pouring straight inside of her. And his movements got faster. He was banging her. He couldn't stop if his life depended on it. It got so good to him that he quickly pulled out, snatched the split condom off of his penis, and shoved his cock back inside of her.

Janet felt the rawness of his penis too. And she didn't want him to stop either. And he kept doing her, and she kept having rolling orgasms. Until neither one of them had anything left.

And then Richard finally stopped his gyrations and eased out of her. And he looked at her. When he saw that she was smiling that wonderful bright white smile on that adorable face of hers, confirming for him that it did get better for her, he exhaled. And smiled too.

Janet traced her finger along his square jaw when he smiled. She was so pleased she could hardly believe it. After that initial flurry of painfulness, she had felt the sensations too. She knew it, and he knew it too. He could see it all over her glowing face. He felt her excitement.

But he also felt ashamed. Why did he take her to that emotional high when he knew he wasn't going to stay there with her? Why did he do that to her? He wasn't helping her. He was hurting her!

And he'd robbed her too.

He rolled off of her, got up, and sat on the edge of the bed. He began putting back on his clothes.

Janet pulled her wide-open rode closed again, but she knew her body would never feel the same again. What Richard had done to her was so beyond her wildest imaginings of how her first time would be that it bore no resembled to what she had in mind. He blew her away. She'd never felt so wonderful, and so alive, in her life.

But did he feel it too? He seemed upset to her as he put back on his clothes. Then he found that condom he had discarded, grabbed it, and looked at her. "I'm going to the men's room," he said. "Get dressed."

"It's still too early for you to take me to work. And I told you I need to get used to my routine."

"Not for that," Richard said. "We need to go by All Night." All Night was a drugstore in town that never closed. They were open twenty-four hours a day, seven days a week.

But Janet didn't understand. "Why would we need to go there?"

"The morning after pill," he said.

Janet was confused. "What's that?" she asked.

Richard just stood there. He couldn't believe it. He didn't just rob her of her body. He robbed her of her innocence. She was a twenty-two-year-old kid who never had to think about morning after pills, and he should have known that! And he could hardly stand himself. All those women at his disposal, and he had to go and ruin her life! What was wrong with him?!

"It'll prevent an unwanted pregnancy," he explained to her.

When he said it was when Janet realized the implications of what they'd done. Not for once did she consider any ramifications. It seemed like the natural course of events for Richard to take her virginity. Somebody was going to, and she had no prospects at all. It just seemed natural to her. Even when he removed

PLAIN JANE EVANS AND THE BILLIONAIRE

that condom, she wasn't thinking about consequences. She was thinking how he must be enjoying it too! But she could be pregnant. He could have passed some incurable disease to her. She became stricken with fear.

They had the fun. Now it was time for them to face the consequences of their action.

"I'll be ready," she said to him, and got out of bed.

He gave her a hard look that she couldn't read, and then he went to the men's room to dispose of his crime.

CHAPTER EIGHT

She watched as he went into that drugstore a purchased those morning after pills. In that fancy suit he wore, he looked so out of place in a factory town like Cope. But that was the first man she'd ever been with, a man like that. And it was a lot for her to process.

When he got back into his car that was parked in front of the drugstore, with the pills and a bottled water, he watched as she took the pills.

"You're okay?" he asked her as he started the car.

She nodded. "I'm okay."

"I don't want you worrying," he said. "Those pills will take care of it, alright?"

"Alright."

"And you needn't worry about contracting any STD."

Janet looked at him.

"I never have unprotected sex," he explained. "I don't know what happened, but that was my first condom break. My very first one. I didn't think that shit was real when other guys talked about it. But when I was with you? Damn, girl," he added with a smile.

Janet laughed.

"So I'm clean, alright?" Richard reassured her. "You needn't worry."

Janet nodded. "That's good to hear," she said, but she still couldn't believe she had allowed him to do her raw.

"Don't you dare feel guilty," Richard said to her when he saw that look on her face. "You did nothing wrong. You hear me? Nothing."

Janet nodded, but he could tell she was still upset.

Which only made him feel worst. "Let's get you to work," he said, putting his car in gear.

And this time, Janet didn't object. After what they'd done, their relationship was on an entirely different level now. And she had to let him treat her right. And right treatment meant he wasn't going to have her waiting at a bus stop. He was going to take her to work, and she was going to let him.

At least that was how she felt about it. She kept glancing over at Richard as he drove. His face gave nothing away. She couldn't figure out how he felt.

When they arrived at the mill, it was super-early. Only a few minutes after five.

"What time does it open?" Richard asked her.

Janet smiled. "You don't know what time your own mill opens?"

"Sweetheart, I'm not that kind of hands-on owner. I put excellent people in charge and expect them to do their jobs."

Janet smiled. Not so much about the fact that he was a bad owner who didn't keep tabs on his own business, but because he called her sweetheart. Her head was in that space, that emotional space, on that particular morning. "It opens at six," she said, and was about to get out.

"What are you doing?" he asked, stopping her. "I'm not leaving you here alone."

"I'm going across the street," she said, pointing over there. "That's where they told us we can wait if we get to work early."

Richard looked across the street and saw an open-all-night truck-stop café. He could see that other workers, the early birds, were waiting inside too. He hadn't even noticed the place when he came to the mill's dedication on yesterday. "Let me take you over there," he said and drove across the street.

"Thanks," she said, getting ready to get out of his car.

"You'll be okay then?" he asked her.

"Oh, yes. Thank you."

But he still looked distressed to Janet. "Take care of yourself, Janet," he said to her.

She smiled. "You too, Richard."

She lingered, hoping he would ask her out or ask if he could come over again, but he didn't say anything else. But he did give her a hug.

He didn't know why he did it. Why was he hugging her for crying out loud? Maybe it was the guilt kicking his butt. She felt so small, so fragile in his arms. He closed his eyes as he held her.

And when she got out of his car, he felt two feet tall.

But as Janet walked into that café, she felt ten feet tall. She was in a state of bliss. In one morning she knew what all the fuss was about. Thanks to Richard. Her dream come true. And she was happy!

And even after Richard sped off, and after she paid for a cup of coffee and sat at a window table inside that café, she couldn't stop smiling. He held her. He held her all night. And made love to her that morning. That was everything! The first time she'd had company inside her room, the first time she made love, was with somebody like Richard Shetfield! That felt good. Because he was good. Because he was the nicest man she'd ever met, hands down, even though he didn't think he was nice at all. But he'd been nothing but good to her.

And although he made no plans about

getting together again, she knew he would. That, to her, went without question. She couldn't wait to see him again.

CHAPTER NINE

Later that same day, while she was hard at work at the mill, Lance Colvin, her line supervisor, was shocked. He was outside staring at the guy as if the guy were from Mars. He was just that stupefied.

"Will you go get her please?" the man asked. Again.

But Lance was still reeling. *Her,* he kept saying to himself. He chose *her?*

He apparently had. And the guy was waiting.

Lance went back inside, went to the work floor, and called her name. "Evans!" he yelled over the sounds of roaring machines. "Evans!"

Janet was at the spinner when Lance called her name. "Yes, sir, Boss?" she yelled back.

"Come with me!"

Lance didn't wait for her to let him know if she could drop everything at that moment. He just left. And Janet, knowing how angry he would get whenever he wasn't obeyed and obeyed in a hurry, got in a hurry and followed him off of the floor and out of the exit doors.

"What's this about, Boss?" she asked him

as they exited the building.

"That's what it's about," he said.

Janet was still wiping her hands on her full-length apron when he motioned with his hand. She looked where he was motioning, but she didn't see anything out of the ordinary. "What?" she asked him.

"What do you mean what?" Lance said impatiently. "That car! It's yours."

Janet was astounded. She looked again, at the pearl-white Mercedes parked in the parking lot, with a smiling white man standing beside it. She had assumed it was his car, and he was there on his own business.

"And it ain't no bottom of the line Mercedes, either," Lance said. "That's an S-class. It's the top of the line Mercedes." He looked at her with nothing short of disgust in his eyes. "What on earth did you do to get yourself a car like that?" he asked her.

But Janet was too amazed to even consider the implications of what Lance had said. She didn't even hear what he had said. She shook her head. "There's some mistake," she said to him, still staring at that car. "That can't be for me!"

"It is for you. It's yours. That's one of the salesmen from the dealership in Tulsa. He drove it over here. He says the title's in the glove compartment. And it's in your name. Because I asked all of those questions too. I was as shocked as you are." Then he looked at her. "You do know how to drive, don't you?"

"Of course I do." She got her learner's permit when the Henleys needed her to drive for them and run their errands for them. When she turned eighteen and got away from the Henleys, she got a full-fledged license.

But that wasn't her issue. The car was. "But where did it come from?" she asked Lance. "Did I win it, or?"

"No, you didn't win it, you idiot! Mr. Shetfield bought it for you."

For the first time since that car came into the frame, Janet looked away from that car, and at Lance. "Richard?" she asked.

Lance gave her a disgusted look. "Yeah. *Richard*. Your boyfriend I assume. He gave it to you."

He was hardly her boyfriend! But she ignored Lance and looked back at that car. And she actually smiled. Now it made sense to her. He didn't want her walking home in the dark ever again, nor going to work in the dark the way she almost did that very morning. And suddenly it seemed wonderful to her, and not at all confounding.

But a Mercedes? "How am I supposed to

afford the upkeep on a car like that?" she asked.

"You'll manage. Because that car right there? Easily worth a hundred thousand."

Janet's eyes grew larger. "A hundred *what*?"

"I told you it's an S class, girl. Easily worth that much." Then he tossed the keys to her. "Look inside. Check it out. Then get your ass back on the line," Lance said, and went back inside. But not before giving her another disgusted look, and shaking his head.

But Janet wasn't thinking about Lance. She was still too stunned. She could hardly believe it. The idea that Richard would purchase her a car, period, was exciting. The idea that he would purchase her a one-hundred-thousand-dollar car was another planet!

She walked over to the car and spoke to the salesman. "That's right," he said. "It's yours, young lady. Thanks to Mr. Shetfield."

"But . . . Did he say anything or?"

"Say? What's there to say? You own this beautiful automobile!" Then the salesman did remember something. "Oh, yes, he did give me something else." He reached into a folder he was carrying and pulled out a newspaper clipping. "He told me to give you this."

Janet took the clipping and saw that it was the picture of a beautiful black woman. The caption read: *Janet Evans, cashier at the SafeWay, wins local dance competition. Grand prize: fifty dollars!*

"Janet Evans?" Janet asked.

"He said it was your mother," the salesman said.

Janet's eyes grew larger. "My mother?"

"He said that's the only picture his investigator could find of her anywhere," the salesman said.

"But my mother's name was Katira," Janet said, confused.

"That is her name. But her nickname is Janet. Or was. She's apparently deceased."

"Yes," Janet said, still staring at that photograph. "Yes, she is."

"But they called her Janet, by her middle name. That's what most people knew her by. It's in the article."

Janet read the article about the hometown girl wining the fifty-dollar prize. And she smiled. It was a grainy photo, but it represented the only picture of her mother she had ever seen. And Richard got it for her. "How did he find it?" she asked, still staring at that photo.

"He hired an investigator apparently," said the salesman. "Doesn't take long these days, not with computers and such."

Janet understood that. She'd tried searching for pictures of her mother online, too, but found absolutely nothing.

"Anyway," the salesman said, "I'm here mainly to show you how it works."

Janet finally looked away from her mother's picture. "How what works?"

"This car, young lady!"

Janet had to smile herself. She had forgotten all about that car!

And as the salesman attempted to show her how to operate a Mercedes, and even as she sat inside of the beautiful car, it was Richard that was driving her happiness. The red leather seats with the white piping. The wood grain finish even on the doors. That new car smell she'd always heard about! She was over the moon.

Because of Richard. That excitement she felt whenever she was in his presence, had apparently been reciprocated. He was excited too. Why else would he buy her a luxury car? Why else would he hire an investigator to see if he could find a photograph of her mother?

She couldn't wait to thank him when she saw him again!

But she didn't see him again. Not that day. Not the next day. Not the day after that.

She didn't even have his phone number to call him, and he certainly didn't try to get in touch with her. It was baffling to her. And painful. It was like she was told she was about to go on the trip of a lifetime, and she did all the prep work for the trip, only to find out that the trip was canceled.

When she asked Lance if he'd heard from Richard, just to make sure he was okay, Lance gave her startling news. "Why would I hear from him?" he asked. "He went back home the day he gave you that car. But I did just get the word."

Janet was confused. "What word?"

"Don't play dumb with me. Give me some credit."

"Lance, what are you talking about? What word?"

Lance looked at her. She didn't know? "Mr. Shetfield called the mill manager."

Janet was pleased to hear that. "So he's alright then?" she asked.

"Yes, he's alright," Lance said. "Why wouldn't he be alright?"

"Then what word are you talking about?"

"Mr. Herman, the assistant mill manager, you may have heard, has gotten a promotion to another Shetfield company somewhere in Ohio."

"I didn't hear it, but okay."

"Yeah, I forgot. You're a frontline worker. Why would you hear about management changes? But that apparently opened the door for you."

Janet was still confused. "For me?"

"Once Mr. Herman clears out in two weeks' time, you will become the new assistant mill manager. You will become the second highest ranking person at the whole mill." Then Lance gave her another disgusted look. "Lil' ol' you," he said.

Janet was floored. "Mr. Shetfield did that for me?"

"He did. I wonder why?" he asked sarcastically. "I just got the word."

"But . . ." Janet didn't know what to say. What on earth did she know about managing a mill? She was only twenty-two years old and barely knew how to work on the floor! What was Richard thinking? And why wasn't he telling her all of this himself?

Then she thought about what Lance had said about his home. "You said he went back home," she said. "What do you mean?"

Lance didn't see where it was hard to understand what he said. "I meant what I said," he said. "He went back home."

"To Tulsa?"

"Tulsa? He has a house there, sure. But I'm talking Europe. Don't you know anything? Don't you know lover boy lives in Europe?"

Janet was floored. Richard lived in *Europe*? Was that why he didn't tell her himself about the car, and that crazy promotion? He wasn't even in America anymore?

Lance smiled. "You had no idea, did you?"

It was obvious by the stricken look on her face that she didn't. Then Lance's smile left. He wasn't a kind man, but he wasn't a sadistic one either. He saw the pain in Janet's eyes. She wasn't used to this. "Get back to work, Evans," he said to her. "For a man like Shetfield to give a fancy car to a woman, or a big promotion is no big deal. It's just like giving a box of candy to a woman for the rest of us guys. It means nothing to him. Get back to work."

And Janet did just that. She got back to work. But for the remainder of that whole day, and the rest of that whole week, she was in a daze.

Her coworkers had been whispering about her relationship with Richard, and his extravagant gift, ever since he gave her that car. She didn't care at the time, because she thought. . . She thought what? The fact that he had given her a car said everything about their relationship? Only to discover it said nothing about their relationship because there wasn't a relationship. Because he had left for Europe, without so much as telling her that he was leaving, that very same day!

And when word spread about her possible promotion to assistant manager, those rumors became vicious and overwhelming. Everybody was talking!

She felt like a fool. And she wasn't angry at Richard. He'd been nothing but kind to her. How could she be angry at the man who found a picture of her mother for her? She was angry with herself. She knew better than to let herself get carried away by a brief moment in time. But she had done just that. She had not only allowed her heart to hope, but she had allowed herself to put her hope in somebody so beyond her reach that it was like reaching, not just for the stars, but for the sky, too, while she was at it. And that ache she felt for days, for the loss of someone she never had to lose, was exactly what she deserved.

And at lunch time, she knew what she had to do. She went straight to Lance's office.

"Give that car back to him," she said, handing him the keys.

But Lance wouldn't accept them. "Give it back?" He had a fixed frown on his face. "It's in your name, Evans. There's no giving it back! You should not have given it up."

Janet looked at him. She understood exactly what he meant. "I didn't give anything up!" she said angrily.

"Yeah, sure. He just gave you an S-class because he likes you. He just made you assistant manager because you're so intelligent. Sure buddy. Nobody at this mill believes that! Ask your coworkers. They're talking about you like a dog. They're talking how you slept your way to that car, and to that promotion. They're saying you have no shame."

Janet was stunned. She knew the talk was crazy, but she didn't realize how true they must have believed it was.

"Although," Lance continued, "why he would want to get it from somebody like you is a mystery to me. All these good-looking birds around this mill and he picks you? Now that's surprising. But that's not my problem, is it? Now get out of my face and get back on the line!"

"I'm on my lunch break."

"Then go on to lunch! Just get away from me!"

By week's end, she quit her job. The rumor mill was running so rampant that nobody believed a word she said. It was as if one day she was a good Christian girl with solid Christian morals, and the next day she was a trash-barrel whore. It was crippling.

No way was she going to allow her boss or her coworkers or anybody else to think of her as somebody's whore. Especially somebody who didn't have the decency to at least let her know he would not be hanging around. Not that he said he would anyway. She knew he never so much as hinted that he would. But she had thought that car gift said it all. And her mother's photograph. And then that promotion? Why would he take such drastic measures if she meant nothing to him?

Probably because he could, she decided.

She had no job waiting somewhere else. She barely had enough money saved to last a good two months. But she quit anyway. Her reputation, and her character, were trashed at the mill, and she couldn't live in that. Her self-respect was worth more to her than even a roof over her head. That was why she quit.

Her nice old landlady said she should give back that car too. "Don't ever let a man buy your affections, young lady," she said to Janet, "or you'll never be free."

But Janet knew that wasn't true either. Richard wasn't trying to buy her affections at all. He didn't want her affections. He just didn't want her to walk to work in the dark. That was it. That was all of it. But realizing that was all there was to it disappointed Janet mightily, and it led her into weeks of irrational hurt and shame. Until she was fully able to face reality. Richard's intentions were good. It was the rest of the world, and Janet too, who misunderstood.

She kept her mother's photograph. But she returned that car.

Although that situation could have broken her, she refused to let it write her story. She hit the pavement running, not whining. And she searched for work everywhere they were taking applications. Gas stations. McDonalds. Clothing stores. Burger King. The chicken factory. The Piggly Wiggly. A janitorial service. Anywhere and everywhere.

And it paid off. By month's end, she found a new position. At Rooney and Rice, a consulting firm. It was another minimum wage, entry-level job at a brand-new company too. But at least it was an office job with room for advancement. At least it was a new beginning. At least the Shetfields didn't own it.

She felt as if she had failed up.

The next time she saw Richard; the first time she understood what it truly meant to love

and to be loved, would occur six years later.
But not a moment too soon.

CHAPTER TEN

SIX YEARS LATER
Three Weeks Before Christmas

"Bells will be ringing,
the glad, glad news.
Oh, what a Christmas
to have the blues.
My baby's gone;
I have no friends
to wish me greetings,
ooh, once again.

Choirs will be singing, 'Silent Night.'
Christmas carols. By candlelight.
Please come home for Christmas.
Please come home for Christmas.
If not for Christmas,
by New Year's night."

He was home for Christmas and the stereo was blaring *Please Come Home for Christmas*, a Charles Brown tune. But even back home in Tulsa, where he had no intentions of staying any longer than he had to, it felt just as lonely as Paris.

He stood behind his room-sized bar, a lit cigar between his fingers, and poured himself another glass of wine. The bright light was blinking on his answering machine, and the digital display showed that he had nine calls waiting. Which confounded him. He didn't announce his arrival. Why so many calls?

He didn't feel like bothering, but he pressed the button anyway.

Beep.

"Dicky, why haven't you phoned me? They said at the club you were spotted in town. Give me a call!"

Beep.

"Dick darling! You're back in town? That's great news! Give me a ring and we'll do something special. And you know what I mean. L.O.L."

Beep.

"Hey baby. I heard you were back. It's all the rave at the club. How long this time? I've missed you. Give me a buzz and I promise to give you one!"

The "club" was his country club. A place where the town's elites went to hang out together and hide out from the commoners when it was the commoners, in Richard's view, who probably needed the respite from them. He hated that club, with all the backslapping and phoniness and glad-handing. But ever since he decided to make his own way, apart from the family oil business, it was expected of him to at least show up.

But he rarely did what was expected of him.

Except, he thought to himself, when it came to Janet.

He drank more wine and took a long drag on his cigar. And just like every time when he was back home in Oklahoma, his mind went back to Janet Evans. He wondered if she would be one of the women leaving him a message. But he knew she never would. The only woman he would actually call back was the only woman who wouldn't call him to begin with. Because she wasn't that kind of girl.

He remembered, six years ago, when the owner of that Mercedes dealership phoned him. He had just left Tulsa earlier that week and was at his chateau in Paris, in bed, with some woman whose name he wasn't sure he ever knew. It was ten o' clock in the morning, but being the party-person he was whenever he was back home in Paris, he and his lady friend were still asleep.

He opened his eyes and looked at his cell phone on the nightstand. Ten am. He remembered wondering who would phone him that time of morning. But he answered anyway.

"Yes?" His voice was husky and barely discernible. It had to be obvious to whomever was on the other end that he had been asleep.

"Sorry to disturb you, Mr. Shetfield."

"Who is this?"

"It's Michael, sir. Michael Greer."

Richard exhaled. He knew him. He knew he owned that Mercedes dealership in Tulsa, and that he was a friend of one of his brothers. But why would he be calling him that time of morning? "What is it?" he asked him.

"To my own astonishment, sir, she returned the vehicle."

Richard frowned. "Who returned what vehicle?"

"Miss Janet Evans, sir. She returned the S-class."

Richard heard it, but he couldn't believe it. She *returned* it? Who returns a Mercedes?

It was enough for him to throw the covers off of his naked body, swing his legs out, and sit on the edge of his bed. His lady friend stirred. "Dicky," she said, reaching for him, "come back to bed!"

But Janet was on his mind. "What did she say when she returned it?" he asked Greer.

"She said it didn't belong to her. She said to please give it back to you."

Richard frowned again. "That's all she said?"

"That's all she said. My lot manager tried to reason with her, of course. But he was so blown away, too, that he couldn't find the words to say. You've given many cars to many ladies since I've owned that dealership. And I thank you for the business. She was the absolute first, in all my years, who returned one."

It was a first for Richard too. But it confirmed what he had suspected all along. She just wasn't that kind of girl! She had the kind of morals that people like him would say were fanatical. Because the morals of people like him depended on the situation. Her morals never changed. They were her way of life.

And he took her virginity. That sweet girl. What an asshole!

But then he remembered a surge of excitement shooting through his body when he had actual confirmation that Janet was who he thought she was. Could he have finally found the kind of lady he always wanted to have, but just knew could never exist? Could she really be the true definition of a good woman? He was so excited that his first inclination was to take the first plane.

But then he thought about why he didn't phone her after that morning in the first place. It wasn't because she was a bad girl. It was because she was good! It was because he saw just how fragile she was, and how sweet she was, and how his slick ass wasn't about to play with her emotions and mess her up. She couldn't handle a man like him. And he knew, deep down, that he couldn't handle a woman like her.

And the reality of it. That he had found a good woman that he wasn't good enough to have, sent him into that downward spiral of depression he sometimes found himself caught up in. He even told Greer to hold on as he stood up, his cell phone still in his hand, and walked away, with his lady friend yelling for him to stay. *"Dicky!"* she yelled in her own sleepy voice. *"Come back to bed, Dicky*!"

But he ignored her. He needed a drink. He went into the parlor that was adjacent to his bedroom, where a full-sized bar was housed, poured himself a stiff one, and then picked back up his cell phone. "What about the photograph?" he asked Greer.

"Oh, you are so right, sir," Greer said. "I almost forgot. She did keep the photograph actually. And she told my manager to thank you for that."

At least he didn't completely blow it in her eyes, Richard thought.

"What do you want me to do with the vehicle, sir?" Greer asked him.

Richard took another sip of his drink.

"Sir?"

And it was Greer's impatience that gave him a license to take his frustration out on the dealership owner. Although even he knew his anger had nothing to do with that poor man. "What the fuck you think you're going to do with it?" he asked Greer. "You're going to keep your car and refund me my money. That's what you're going to do with it!" And Richard ended the call. And angrily tossed his phone onto the bar counter.

He remembered wondering why was he so angry? It wasn't like he needed another woman in his life. He had too many already.

But none of them, not one, was anything like Janet.

But he wasn't anything like her either. That was why he was having such a strong reaction to a woman he barely knew. Because he wasn't worthy to get to know her better. He wanted to. Lord knows how much he wanted to! He felt his life would never be anything more than lurching from woman to woman, from obscenity to obscenity, until he made himself worthy of a good woman's love. Something he didn't even know how to do. And he remembered drinking too much that morning, and thinking how it was such a shame.

And then he found out, when his management team phoned to brief him on the progress of the mill that Janet Evans turned down the promotion to assistant manager and then quit altogether. Which shocked him. Why on earth would she had quit her job?

And it was only then did he realize how his offer could have been so badly misconstrued, not only by her, but by the people she worked with too. Did they think a good girl like her was sleeping her way to the top? What else were they going to think when he suddenly gives a Mercedes to a minimum wage worker and a job promotion that would make her the second most powerful person at the entire mill?

He felt awful when he realized his blunder. Just awful! And he wanted to correct the error. But how? Tell already doubtful people that it wasn't true? That she would never sleep her way to the top? They'd believe for certain that it was absolutely true if he made such a big deal out of it that way. He knew then, even more than he already knew, that he had to leave that good lady alone.

But that was six years ago. Why was he thinking about Janet Evans right now, six years later? Because his dumbass blew his one chance at finding true love with his extravagant gifts and foolishness, and blew up her life in the process? Could that be it?

He stood behind his bar in his home in Tulsa, Oklahoma, three weeks before Christmas, and drained the rest of the liquor in his glass.

Beep.

He listened to another message. This one from Doris Wilson, his longtime secretary.

"Hello, Boss. This is your beloved Doris calling. When you get in town give me a ring pretty-please. I've scheduled the consulting firm just as you requested, and they'll be at the office tomorrow morning, nine am sharp. But isn't this something? Three weeks before Christmas and we've got to deal with this crap again. It's just awful the way people do you! I still say we should call in the lawyers and be done with it, rather than bringing in P.R. people, but your wish is my command. I am at your service. You wanted P.R., so P.R. is what you got. Tomorrow. Nine am. See you then!"

But when another female came on after Doris's voice mail, he put an end to the remaining calls altogether, and deleted them all.

He walked over to his expansive window and looked out over the dark, foreboding lake that fronted his backyard. Part of the reason he was back in town was because of another harassment complaint against his mill, but this time with a group of women making the allegations. Which wasn't unusual for a mill that size. That was why he was advised by the lawyers to settle out of court the last three times, which he reluctantly did. But such a move, in his view, set a horrible precedent. Now they were tripping over each other with complaints. But he wasn't settling this time. A different precedent needed to be set. He was going to fight.

"Friends and relations,
send salutations.
Sure as the stars shine above.
This is Christmas,
yes, Christmas my dear.
The time of year,
to be,
with the one you love.

Then won't you tell me,
you'll never more roam.
Christmas and New Year,
will find you home.
There'll be no more sorrow,
no grief and pain.
And I'll be happy.

Happy.
Once again."

He took a long drag on his cigar as that haunting guitar hook played over his stereo. *Happy*, the song said. He was thirty-seven years old. No wife. No children. No real life beyond work. And that song was talking about being happy?

What on earth, he wondered, was that?

CHAPTER ELEVEN

Janet placed breakfast on the table and seventy-year-old Morris "Mo" Riley smiled a big, toothy smile. "You're going to make a great wife someday, Baby Girl," he said as he stared down lovingly at those Oklahoma cheese grits, those eggs over-easy, and that country-fried steak he always adored. "Best meal of the day!" he added.

"Remember I'm taking you to your doctor's appointment after work," Janet said as she began stuffing papers into her briefcase. "Be ready to go. We'll only have fifteen minutes to get there."

"Yeah, yeah," Mo said. "We'll get there with a minute to spare the way you always do it. You're the one-minute girl. Always on time, but just by a minute."

Janet laughed. A year after she left the Shetfield textile mill job and established herself at Rooney and Rice, she moved out of her room in that boarding house on Grundy Street and leased an apartment. And then she went searching for Mo Riley. She began where it left off for her: at the little house she moved into when she was four years old. At the house those social workers moved her out of when she was six years old after Mo's wife had died. But he had moved out of that house, too, according to a neighbor, nearly eight years ago.

But Janet kept searching. She went from pillar to post searching at the various rooms he had rented and other places he'd stayed. Until finally she found him whittling away in a poorly run nursing home for the poorest of the poor elderly. The place reeked. He was filthy and severely overmedicated to a point of stupor. And Janet was angry. She told them she was his daughter (she had, after all, once been his foster daughter), and they allowed her to take him with her with no further questions asked. They seemed glad to be rid of him.

She moved him into her apartment, and later into the small house she was now purchasing. He improved immediately, got better as the years came and went, and was now his old self again. He was quite capable of taking care of himself and her beside, as he never ceased to remind her.

"What are we doing for Christmas this year, Baby Girl?" he asked her as he ate.

"Same thing we do every year. Eat and watch basketball."

"And then on Christmas night. You remember, right?"

"Remember what?"

"Janet! I'm going to the casino with the Golden Girls like I do every year!" The "Golden Girls" were his gambling partners. All senior citizens. All retired. All flirty as hell. He loved it because he was the only male in the group.

"Just messing with you," Janet said with a smile. "Yes, I remember. You know I remember. Ethel is driving, right?"

"With her half-blind self, yes, she is," said Mo. "But I'll take the wheel if I have to."

"You don't have a license," Janet said. "You'd better not."

Mo smiled. "Just joking." Then he looked at Janet. "But what about you?"

"What about me?"

"What you gon' do Christmas night while I'm gone?"

"I have this book I plan to read. With you out of the house, I just might get enough uninterrupted time to actually finish it."

"You need a man, Janet," Mo said bluntly.

"Don't start."

"You need a man! When since that became controversial? You're twenty-eight years old. You're gonna be thirty soon."

"I thought I was going to be twenty-nine soon."

"And you never even been on a date with a man before," Mo continued.

Richard crossed Janet's mind. It was six years ago, but could that have been classified as a date?

"You should be dating several men," Mo said.

"Men don't date women who look like me," Janet said bluntly too. "At least not any man around here."

Mo frowned. "Since when a good man don't want to date a good woman?"

"Okay, I stand corrected. They don't want to date me," Janet said.

"Since when?"

"Since all my life, Mo! They don't bother with me. So stop going on and on about something that doesn't matter. Please."

"But why?" Mo asked. "It don't make no sense! You're smart, there's not a lazy bone in your body, and you clean your ass every single day. What more they want? And you're beautiful, too, Janet."

"Don't," Janet said, shaking her head.

"You are beautiful! And a good man will want to date you."

"I'm shovel face. I'm horse face. I'm Plain Jane. Men don't look at me, they look pass me to the other girl. Which is fine. I've resigned myself to that reality when I was still a teenager. I accept that fact. I don't need a man to complete me anyway. I complete myself. My Lord and I," she said with a smile. "So just don't patronize me, okay? Your wife, God rest the dead, was a gorgeous woman herself. Even you wouldn't have dated somebody like me had we been contemporaries, and they don't get any better than you." Then Janet grabbed up her briefcase and keys. "Just be ready for your doctor's appointment," she said to him as she walked over and kissed him on the cheek. Then she hurried to the back door that led outside to the carport.

"You just be here on time," he said to her, "and I'll be ready."

"You know I'll be here," said Janet. "I'd never stand up one of my dearest friends."

"Quit lying," said Mo. "I'm your only friend."

Janet laughed, but hurried on out of the door.

But as soon as that door slammed shut, Mo's smile left. Every night he asked the Lord to keep him on this earth long enough to see Janet happy and in love and ready to start a family. Because he knew she was telling nothing but the truth. And it angered him. Because, back in the day, she wouldn't have been his type either. Great-looking whorish girls, with plenty of street smarts, were his type.

And that was a shame, he knew. Because they didn't make women greater than Janet. What young girl in her early twenties would have searched up some old geezer like him and brought him home to live with her? He should have been forgotten in that nursing home. But Janet didn't forget him. She brought him home with her and kept him with her for the past five years. Because that was the kind of wonderful woman she was. But how in the world were any of those superficial, foolish men ever going to know that if all they could see was the outside, and the inside didn't matter to them? And when even he wouldn't have bothered getting to know somebody like her better, either, back in the day?

He pushed his plate away in frustration. He just didn't want her to end up alone. No husband. No children. No life?

He no longer had an appetite.

CHAPTER TWELVE

She parked her car in the nearly full parking lot, grabbed her briefcase and Dunkin Donuts cup of coffee, and hurried into the front entrance of the Rooney and Rice Consultants office building with just two minutes to spare.

"You time it like a pro," one of her coworkers said jokingly as she hurried to her cubicle. She smiled, although she wasn't pleased. Barely making it to work on time every single day wasn't something to be proud of. Especially since she and Marveen Whitaker and only a handful more were the only African

Americans in the entire company, and appearances did matter. Even though she had yet to be late.

But as soon as she plopped down in her desk chair, one of her coworkers were already calling her name. "Jane? Jane?"

She knew it was going to be about one of them asking her to help them to do this, or show them how to do that. Knowledge was still power in that office, and everybody wanted to pick Janet's brain.

"Jane? *Jane*?" her coworker whispered again.

When she first arrived at Rooney and Rice six years ago, she was Janet Evans to all of her coworkers. And she loved the fact that, just like at her other jobs, she had reclaimed her name that she felt the Henleys had stolen. But a few days into her tenure there, a young lady was hired who knew her from the Henleys' neighborhood. She started calling her Jane since that was the only name she knew her by, and others took up the name too. The girl was fired the very next month, for insubordination, but the nickname stuck. Gone was Janet. She was Jane again. She corrected her coworkers incessantly in the beginning. She would prefer to be called by her Christian name, she'd tell them. And some honored her request. But most never did. Jane was simpler to remember, and seemed to fit better than Janet, one coworker had the nerve to tell her.

"Jane!"

"I heard you the first time. I'm putting up my purse." She placed her purse in the bottom desk drawer in her cubical and then rolled her chair to the cubicle next to hers. Beth Pataki was her best friend at work. And also a big gossip.

"What do you need help with today?" Janet asked her.

"Help? I don't need any help."

Janet was embarrassed that she had assumed too much. "Oh, I'm sorry. I thought. Never mind. What did you want?"

Beth lowered her voice. "Did you hear the news?"

"What news?"

"About Kimmie, girl. She got another raise!"

Kimmie Fisher. Hired three years ago. Janet trained her. Now Kimmie was the unit supervisor. "Didn't she just get a raise last year?" Janet asked.

"That's what I'm telling you," Beth said. "They just gave her another one! We haven't gotten any in years, and they keep handing it over to her lazy butt. But, of course, we aren't sleeping our way to the top."

"Um-hun," said Marveen Whitaker, who sat in the cubicle on the opposite side of Beth, and who agreed with Beth without even showing her face.

Not that they had any proof that the girl was sleeping her way to success. They didn't. But it was the only explanation that they could think of. The alternative, Janet knew, would say too much about them.

From the moment Kimmie was hired there were rumors about her and her sleep partners around the office, but Janet never trafficked in rumors. She left a job over rumors. She, instead, had facts on her side. And the fact was clear: she trained Kimmie. She outperformed Kimmie every single year. Kimmie got the raises. Kimmie got the promotions. Kimmie cozied up to William Rice like he was her man. And she was only one example of all the people who Janet had trained, that were now ahead of her.

After hearing the news that Kimmie continued to be rewarded for her lackluster work performance, it only confirmed for Janet that the decision she made just a few days ago was the absolute right one.

But when she didn't respond to Beth's news and Marveen's amen, Beth looked at her coworker. "Did you hear me? She's getting another raise. What do you have to say about that?"

"What am I supposed to say?" Janet asked. "Because all my raise requests are turned down, I should want hers turned down too? How will that help me?"

"Right is right and wrong is wrong," said Beth.

"That's right," said Marveen from her amen corner. "And two wrongs don't make a right."

"You and me both have been here longer than she has," Beth continued talking to Janet, "and we both have better results with every client we serve. But she gets the raise? She gets the promotion? It's wrong I tell you. It's so unfair!"

But being unfairly treated wasn't news to Janet. That was the story of her life. The news would be if she were treated fairly.

Although, deep down, hearing that news did hurt. But what could she do about it? She had to work for a living. She needed that paycheck. "Welcome to life," she said, slid back behind her own desk, and turned on her computer.

Both Beth and Marveen leaned their chairs back so that they could look each other in the eyes, and then they rolled their eyes. Janet never played along. She always tried to stay above the fray. "But those are the ones," Marveen once told Beth, "that show up for work the next day and shoot everybody in sight. She's as pissed as we are!"

But when the doors opened from the executive office suite, and William Rice, the boss, came hurrying out with Kimmie and another new hire, a brownnoser called Sheldon, Marveen and Beth both quickly rolled their chairs back behind their desks and pretended to be busy.

Janet glanced up when she heard them enter, but she looked back down at her computer screen. Another one of her clients, a local pastor falsely accused of money laundering, had a successful outcome. She was reading how the DA decided to drop the charges.

But if she thought her lack of attention to the boss and his lackeys would be enough for her to read the article in peace, she was mistaken. As William Rice approached her desk, he pointed at her. "You come too, Jane," he said and didn't break his stride. "I can use your insight on this one."

Janet looked up at him. Mo Riley once said she was all eyes because they were so large, and when she was shocked they grew to a whole other level. Did she hear him right?

William looked back at her. "Yes, I'm talking to you," he said. "Come too!"

"Yes, sir," Janet said quickly, grabbed her purse out of the bottom desk drawer, and hurried behind the boss too. Four people on one case? It had to be a big one.

Beth and Marveen knew it too. They looked over their cubicle walls at Janet, and then rolled their chairs back to look at each other. Why didn't they get selected? They never got selected to go on a case with the big man, not ever! But Janet got to go?

Now Janet was in their crosshairs too.

"Ain't that some bull?" Marveen said.

CHAPTER THIRTEEN

William Rice drove into the parking lot at the Shetfield Office complex in downtown Tulsa, Oklahoma and stopped his car. Then he turned to Kimmie, who sat on the front passenger seat, and then to Janet and Sheldon, who sat in the back. "I'm sure all of you have heard of the Shetfields."

Janet stared at William. She most definitely had heard of the Shetfields! But what did they have to do with them?

"Of course we've heard of them," said Kimmie. "They own most of the state."

"And Texas, too, from what I hear," said Sheldon.

"That's right," said William. "They're big in Texas too. And Richard Shetfield, at least here in Oklahoma, is at the top of that food chain."

Janet's heart began to pound. Richard Shetfield? She was about to meet Richard again?

"He's the one who's giving us this chance to represent him," William continued.

Sheldon smiled. "You mean he's hired us?" he asked.

"Not yet, no," said William. He was the younger of the two men who owned Rooney and Rice, and he was a hot shot who, as Mo Riley would say, thought more of himself than he ought. But he knew how to rope in their biggest clients. "That's what this meeting is about," he continued. "We've got to earn his business."

Janet was stunned. She was about to see Richard again? After all these years of never seeing one hint of him? It seemed surreal to her now.

"Why would he want to hire a firm from Cope," asked Sheldon, "when he could have easily chosen one of the major consulting firms right here in Tulsa?"

"Because the problems he's having involves his textile mill here in Cope," said William.

Janet remembered that mill. She worked there for just one week once upon a time.

"What problems are they having at the mill?" Kimmie asked.

"Lawsuit threats over harassment of some sort. His assistant wouldn't give me the details. But we're about to find out," William added, as he began unbuckling his seat belt.

"Why didn't you tell us sooner, Billy?" Kimmie asked and Sheldon immediately elbowed Janet. And Janet knew why. It was because Kimmie called the boss *Billy*. Because that was how personal their relationship had become. But for Janet, that was their business. Mo always told her: "Stay out of white folks' business." And she did.

"Had you told us sooner," Kimmie continued, "we could have been better prepared."

"That's why I didn't tell you. I don't want you better prepared," William said. "He'll see right through those preparations. He doesn't like to hear rehearsed pitches. That's a well-known fact. He wants a straight answer to whatever question he asks us, not some three-point presentation response."

"He wants us to fly by the seat of our pants," Janet said with a smile, trying to ease her own discomfort, and Sheldon laughed.

But William gave her a hard, cold look through his rearview mirror. "He doesn't want your ass to do anything," he said to her angrily. "You just keep your mouth shut. If I'm not talking, Kimmie will talk. He has a thing for beautiful women, and Kimmie's the only one in this car who fits that bill. You're only here to give me insight after the fact, not during it. You watch and you listen. That's all you will be doing. You feel me? Isn't that how you people say it? You feel me?"

Then William got out of the car. Kimmie got out with a grin on her face. She loved her elevated status.

But when Sheldon and Janet got out of the backseat and began walking behind the boss and their supervisor, he leaned toward Janet. "He's an asshole," he said to her in a low voice, his blue eyes filled with compassion. "Don't let him get to you."

"Me? Never," Janet said with a smile, although his putdowns hurt her to her core. But she wasn't about to let anybody, least of which William Rice and Kimmie Fisher, see her sweat.

Besides, she was about to see Richard again. That had her sweating enough.

And true to form, as soon as they walked into the massive building, she focused exclusively on the job at hand. Her job was to be the observer of the action, to see what the principals might have missed. Despite her boss and his arrogance, she was going to do her job.

The Shetfields of Oklahoma were legendary. She'd heard about them all her life. And most of it was bad. Bad working conditions at their oil refineries, at their factories, at their newspapers, at their sporting goods stores. Paid slave wages she was told, even though Janet knew there was no such thing since slaves weren't paid any wages. But they supposedly treated their workers as if they were their slaves.

She worked for them for all of one week. A new hire making minimum wage. And she quit inside a week when Richard bought her a car, left town, and left her reputation in tatters. She slept her way to that car, was the biggest rumor. The one that felt like a sucker punch every time she stepped onto that factory floor. And Janet couldn't live in that. She was young and poor back then, and needed that job desperately, but nobody was going to try to assassinate her character while she hung around to give them the bullet. She didn't hang around. She couldn't. But Richard's actions, though harmful to her reputation, were well-intentioned, and through the years she always reminded herself of that fact.

"Don't work for the Shetfields," the Henleys used to tell their children. "They're like vampires in suits. They'll suck the life out of you. They'll suck you dry."

One of those vampires sucked her dry. But that was her fault.

Now she was a part of the team that just might represent that same vampire in whatever he needed representation for. It was all so surreal to Janet!

Just as their office complex was too. She'd seen it hundreds of times as she drove around Tulsa looking for work. Sometimes she thought about Richard whenever she saw that building, and that night they had dinner together, and that fateful morning. But other times he didn't cross her mind.

But as they entered the lobby, she felt as if she had stepped into another world. From the massive Christmas tree that nearly touched the high ceiling, to the decorations that overwhelmed the beautiful, busy space, it was a sight to behold. The decorations were so expansive that they bordered on gaudy to Janet based on the sheer volume alone, but that was probably tastefully done to most everybody else. She wouldn't know about things like that anyway. Christmas for her was a quiet dinner at home with Mo.

"Good morning."

When they turned around, a beautiful black woman with a bouffant hairdo was standing in front of them. And she was extending her hand to William. "Mr. Rice, welcome," she said to him as they shook hands. "I'm Doris Wilson. I'm Mr. Shetfield's secretary. Right this way, please."

If his secretary was any indication, William was right. Richard had a thing for beautiful women. Because Doris Wilson put the *g* in gorgeous. Doris Wilson even made Kimmie look plain.

So much so that Sheldon gave Janet another elbow, when they both saw the jealousy coming out of Kimmie like shards of glass.

William apparently saw it too. He placed his hand on Kimmie's back as they, and Sheldon and Janet, followed the secretary down a long corridor that led to a conference room at the end of the hall.

"Mr. Shetfield will be with you shortly," Doris said, and then walked out of the room and closed the double-door behind her.

William smiled and rubbed his hands together as if they were at a blackjack table in Vegas. "Now this is what I call a room," he said, admiring the spacious conference room. "Everybody take a seat. And remember what I said," he added, glancing mostly at Janet.

They were seated for a mere couple of minutes when the door opened again and the man himself, Richard Shetfield, walked in.

And Janet thought she was going to fall out of that chair as soon as he walked through that door. Because that warm feeling she felt the first time she laid eyes on him came flooding back. And the memories of that night, and that fateful morning.

Her second impression of Richard, even after all those years, was still a wow.

CHAPTER FOURTEEN

Not because of his good looks. That would have never wowed her in and of itself. Although she'd admit he was still a very good-looking man. But he wasn't as fun-looking as he had been. Now he was all business. Now he was good-looking but only if you liked the stern, blunt, *let's just get on with it* kind of person. She didn't. She preferred a man with manners.

But what wowed her most about Richard Shetfield, just like before, was his eyes. They were so large and so stark, but yet so desperately sad and kind, that Janet wondered how anybody could describe him any other way. If they were looking at his manners alone, yes, he would be that vampire he and his family were described as. She could see him sucking the life right out of you, and your livelihood while he was at it. But if they were looking at *him*, they

126

couldn't help but see a man who might have been as horrible and shallow as they said he was, but he wasn't enjoying it. Janet saw that right off. His eyes gave it away.

At least that was how Janet saw him. William and Kimmie and even Sheldon seemed to see his fierce style only, and his crude manners, and they couldn't get beyond that very salient point. That was why they all rose to their feet when he walked in. Janet, however, remained seated. Not because she was being disrespectful. She was still too shocked to stand.

Richard noticed the one who didn't stand immediately on entering the room, and he wondered why she didn't stand. He was accustomed to people standing whenever he entered a room. Especially people who wanted to be on his payroll. That was just how it was done. But she didn't bother.

"You may be seated," he said as he stood at the head of the table like a man accustomed to barking out orders. "As for you," he added, as he looked past Sheldon to Janet, "as you were."

William's eyebrows rose in shock when he realized Janet had not stood up, too, and he looked angrily at her. But he knew how to camouflage better than most. He continued to smile it off as they all, including Richard, sat down.

But as Richard was sitting down, a sharp pang hit him. And then he suddenly realized who she was. The one who didn't stand up. He knew her!

Janet? Was that *Janet*?

"First of all, Mr. Shetfield," William began talking, "I want to thank you for giving us this opportunity to meet with you."

"My secretary gave you the opportunity," said Richard crudely, although his eyes kept darting over at Janet to make sure he was seeing who he thought he was seeing. "That's how you got this meeting. Doris looked you up. She said you're the largest consulting firm in Cope. I suspect you're the only consulting firm in Cope."

Janet smiled. Sheldon and Kimmie looked at William to see if it was safe to smile. When William smiled, too, they did as well. But Richard noticed how the woman in the nice skirt suit, the one who didn't bother to stand, *Janet*, didn't wait for permission. He liked that.

"We aren't the only firm in Cope," William said. "There are quite a few actually. But we like to think we're the best one in Cope."

"Why should I hire Rooney and Rice?" Richard asked. He was doing all he could to keep it together. He couldn't count the times, after he spent that night in her room, after that morning when they made love, when he wanted to throw caution to the wind and go see her again. She was his standard-bearer. She was the shining example to him of what a good woman was. The problem? He wasn't a good man. He didn't deserve her.

"Well, sir," William said, attempting to answer his question, "you should hire Rooney and Rice for a number of reasons."

"Please don't let one of them be because both names begin with an R too."

William frowned. He didn't get the joke. But Janet did. She smiled at that one, too, which made Richard inwardly smile. With her, he was two for two.

Then William caught on. "Oh!" he said. "You mean we're Rooney and Rice and you're Richard. All begin with R. Got it. But no, sir, not at all."

"Then why should I hire you?" Richard took another peep at Janet.

"As I stated, you should hire us for a number of reasons. We are--"

"You're Rooney or Rice?" Richard asked him.

"I'm Rice, sir," William said. Janet could tell he was getting a little perturbed by Richard's constant interruptions. "I'm William Rice. And you should hire our firm because we will represent your interest in a way that places you as our number one priority."

"As would every consulting firm in America," Richard fired back. "I'm a billionaire. At least that's what the papers say. You think I'll let you make me your number two priority?"

Janet smiled again. She couldn't help it. He was slinging aces all over the place and putting that obnoxious William Rice in his place while he was at it. Although, she was also a little shocked. He was a *billionaire*?

But Richard noticed that she had smiled at one of his comments again. She understood his sense of humor when most people just found him crude. She hadn't changed at all, which he was pleased to note.

And William hurried to correct his error. "Oh, no, sir," he said, "we would never place you as number two. Nobody would. You're correct. That's not what I'm saying."

"Then what are you saying, Mr. Rice? Why should I hire your firm?"

"Because you will be getting the . . . the best of the best. Phillip Rooney, as you may know, is legendary in our neck of the woods, and he and I will drop everything to work your case exclusively. And, if I may say so myself, we are undeniably the best of the best."

"You're Rooney and Rice of Cope, Oklahoma," Richard fired back. "Get real, okay? Don't try to come off as if you're in the same league as the Lauder Firm in California, or the Trevor Reese firm in Boston, who handles most of my consulting business by the way, or any of the other major players. I'm only giving your small-ass firm a chance because of the delicacy of this matter and the fact that I need local representation. And by local I don't mean Tulsa. I mean Cope, where the allegations were filed. But I'll forget the local flavor in a heartbeat and go with my top guys if you don't come at me better than you're coming right now."

To say Richard Shetfield was fierce, Janet thought, would be a gigantic understatement. He was mean and callous. And maybe even a bully. But it wasn't as if William didn't deserve it. His unprepared butt deserved every lick. Janet was enjoying his verbal beat down. But it was just that Richard seemed to have changed. Those six years since she last saw him seemed to have hardened him even more than he already was.

Not that she knew him like that. She didn't. But that had been her impression of him.

But William continued to fumble. Janet was seated beside Sheldon and across from

William and Kimmie and she could see it all over William's arrogant face. He didn't know how to come back from a beat down by a real man. He didn't know how to fight back when the fight was fair: two titans against each other. He only knew how to beat up on people like Janet and his other frontline workers. People who couldn't fight back because their livelihoods depended on that job he dangled over their heads.

William, instead, turned to Kimmie. And Kimmie, remembering that Richard Shetfield supposedly loved him some good-looking women, turned on the charm as if she were a sudden floodlight in his dark room. She even stood on her feet so that he could see just how attractive, not only her face was, but her body too. And a pang of jealousy swept through Janet.

"You should hire Rooney and Rice, sir, not because we can compete with the big boys," Kimmie said, making certain to push out her big breasts when she said it, "but because we know Cope. And we know what people in Cope will buy, and what they won't buy. And a big boy like the Trevor Reeses of this world coming down here to tell us how it's done? They ain't buying that."

Janet actually looked at Kimmie. Because Kimmie was talking good sense. At least Kimmie was giving Richard something fresh to think about.

But Richard still seemed unmoved to Janet. It was like he knew they were small potatoes and so out of his league that it wasn't even funny. Was he was entertaining them, anyway, for the hell of it?

Which was exactly how Janet felt after he purchased that car for her, and then left America. He had entertained her for a brief moment in time, knowing she was way out of his league, too, for the hell of it.

"Why would Cope buy something different than Tulsa will buy?" Richard asked. "It's only a twenty-minute drive from there to here."

"But it's a world apart," William said, and Janet smiled. She once told Richard the very same thing.

But Richard found his interruption rude. "I'm talking to the lady," he said to William.

Janet could see William's jaw tighten. He seemed so out of his depth!

"Cope and Tulsa are worlds apart," said Kimmie, answering the question. "William is right. But we know what will sell in Cope. It just depends on what kind of harassment that's being alleged."

"Sexual," Richard said without skipping a

beat.

"On your part?"

When Kimmie asked that question, Janet quickly looked at Richard. Not that it mattered, but it would be a shame, she thought, if it did involve him.

But Richard was already shaking his head. "Heavens no," he said. "I haven't seen the inside of that mill since the day I opened it."

Janet stared at him. Not in the last six years? The day they ran into each other? How could he own a mill and not bother to personally check on it in six years? Then, again, she realized he was super-rich. He probably had a hundred businesses he had to check on. A mill in Cope wasn't high on his list.

"I just own the place," Richard continued, making no bones about it. "I have competent, experienced people I trust running that mill."

"Are the so-called victims all females?" Kimmie asked.

"They are, yes."

"Then that's what we'll have to do," said Kimmie. "We'll have to put those women on trial in the court of public opinion, which is right up our alley. Because where I come from, Mr. Shetfield, those females won't stand a chance."

She was up-playing her small town girl appeal at this point, Janet thought. And to good effect, she also realized.

"Because where I come from," Kimmie continued, "they have a saying. A gold digger will say anything to dig your gold. Those women will allege anything to take your gold from you. It's our job to keep it in your pants."

As she said those suggestive words, she glanced down at Richard, although that conference table was blocking his midsection. But they all got the point. And Janet felt the heat. She remembered that same *point* inside of her!

As Kimmie spoke, Richard was looking at Janet, wondering if she remembered his *point*. Wondering if she remembered him at all.

"That's why they're claiming all of this harassment," Kimmie went on. "That's why Cope and Tulsa are worlds apart. Because, in Cope, we know gold diggers when we see them. And a gold digger never mean nothing good. That's why the word itself rhymes with nig---"

She almost said it. Janet was stunned that she almost said it! All those years working with Kimmie and she never saw that side of her. But as Mo said: you never really know people.

Kimmie caught herself. "Bigger," she said. "That's why it rhymes with bigger, because they want a big chunk of your money. Anyway, that's what they say where I come from," she said, and glanced at Janet.

But Richard wasn't impressed. What a nasty bitch, he thought when Kimmie almost said the n-word. Had Janet not been in the room, he was certain she would have felt comfortable enough to outright say it. As if he would go along with that shit. Which meant, to Richard, it would be a cold day in hell before Rooney and Rice got a dime of business from him.

He wondered how Janet, the only person of color in the room, felt about it. He looked past Sheldon, to Janet.

Janet's heart began to beat faster when he looked her way. She remembered him as if they had bumped into each other just yesterday, rather than six years ago. She'd also noticed how he'd been taking peeps at her since the moment he came into the room, but this time he was staring at her. Did he remember her too? "What about you, Miss um . . . um?"

Did he forget ever running into her period, or just her name, she wondered. And she was about to answer his question, to find out, but William beat her to it. "Jane," William said. "Her name is Jane Evans."

"Miss Evans," said Richard, although he absolutely had not forgotten her nor her name. "What about you?" he asked her. "Do you agree with your coworker?"

"I'm her supervisor," corrected Kimmie. "Not her coworker."

Richard frowned. "Who the fuck cares who you are?!" he yelled at Kimmie, showing a flash of out-of-nowhere real anger, which astonished everybody in the room. Vampire, Janet thought, was an amp term for that man!

But Kimmie was hurt by his outburst. She angrily looked at William, expecting that yellowbelly to take up for her. William, to no one's surprise, didn't say a word.

It didn't matter anyway. Richard had already looked away from both of them, and he was still staring at Janet. "What do you have to say about it?" he asked her.

William gave Janet a hard look, as if he were daring her to say anything at all. But the man asked her a question, and she aimed to answer it. "I say you have a major problem on your hands," she said.

Richard's eyebrows lifted, as if he were finally about to get some truth from at least one of them. Because he could already see that whatever William Rice and his obvious girlfriend were selling, Janet Evans wasn't buying. "Why would you call it a major problem? Simply because an allegation was made?"

"Because where I come from," Janet

said, "they have a saying too."

Kimmie and William both rolled their eyes. But Richard was interested. "Which is?" he asked.

"Where I come from," Janet said, "they like to say where there's smoke, there's fire. Or fire done been there."

William frowned. "Please disregard that nonsense," he said to Richard.

But Richard was smiling at that 'nonsense.' And then he broke into laughter. Janet was surprised at how his sad eyes suddenly had a spark in them when he laughed.

But then the laughter ended almost as quickly as it had begun. "Explain," he said to her.

She realized then that he hadn't remembered her at all. Not her name. Not her face. Not *her*. He seemed to have remembered absolutely nothing about that sweet, innocent night they spent together. And that next morning and trip to the drug store. A night and morning that, for a shamefully long time, defined her very existence.

But before she could respond, William again interrupted her. "I really don't think a response like that is worthy of an explanation," he said to Richard. "I don't think it's worth your time, sir."

Although William seemed ambivalent to Richard's quick temper, Janet wasn't. She could see Richard's temper flare again as soon as William said what he thought. "I don't give a fuck what you think," Richard said to William. "So shut the fuck up!"

What an ill-tempered person, Janet thought. She wondered if he was always so crude. And she wondered why that fire never translated into his stark, tired, sad eyes.

But then he turned those eyes to her. "Explain," he said to her again.

"Not for nothing are those women threatening to sue," Janet said.

"Oh, it's for something," said Kimmie, jumping right back into the fray. She was determined to win that contract against all odds, and maybe earn herself a partnership in Rooney and Rice while she was at it. "Maybe it has something to do with the fact that his company just settled a big case involving sexual harassment here in Tulsa," she continued, "and those women in Cope want in on the action. But you didn't know about that, did you?"

Janet looked at Kimmie. She knew good and gosh-darn well that she wasn't briefed at all before being dragged along by William. But she ignored Kimmie's pettiness. "Yes," she said to Richard, "it is suspicious that after your company settles a major case those women suddenly decide to sue you too."

"But where there's smoke, there's fire," Richard said. "Or just smoke," he added.

"Maybe they want your money," Janet said. "Or maybe they have a legitimate complaint of harassment. Or maybe it's both."

But Richard was staring at her. "You're a gut girl, aren't you?" he said to her. "What does your gut tell you, young lady?"

A gut girl? Janet had never heard it said that way before! But it was the truth. She always relied on her own instincts. "It's usually both," she said.

"It's almost never both," William said. "It's always money, Mr. Shetfield, as I'm sure you're well aware."

Richard stared at Janet a moment longer, without even acknowledging that William had said a word to him. They treated her without even a modicum of respect. And she took their bullshit like a pro. That was the Janet he remembered. That resiliency! That innocent view of life when there was nothing innocent about life. He wished to God he had went back to see her all those years ago. He wished to God he would have tried to change his life to make it work. He could have been a husband. A father. He could have had a family of his own.

But all he had was money and power. And an empty bed unless he grabbed some random woman, looking for money and power herself, to help him make it through the night. And then he was empty again.

Janet wasn't empty, but she was getting very uncomfortable. Because he was staring at her with a look she couldn't read. With a look that either seemed to suggest he was considering what all they'd said, or had already dismissed them out of hand.

And then he abruptly rose to his feet. This time all of them, including Janet, stood up too.

And without saying another word, Richard left the room.

They all looked to William. But William's jaw had already tightened, and his face was already turning beet red. He knew exactly why the man walked out. Janet contradicted Kimmie and made it appear as if they didn't have their act together. He knew exactly at whose feet he was putting that failure.

He gave Janet another one of his icy looks, and then he walked out too.

CHAPTER FIFTEEN

On the ride back to Cope, you could slice the tension with a knife. Nobody said a mumbling word. Until William was tired of stewing in his own juices and let Janet have it.

"I told you to keep your trap shut!" he yelled as he drove. "Didn't I tell you to keep that backward-ass mouth of yours shut? Now look what you've done!"

Janet was shocked. "What *I've* done? What did I do?" she asked.

"You opened your mouth," said Kimmie. "And cost us that contract."

Janet frowned. "*I* cost that contract? That's ridiculous! The man asked me a question and I answered it. What else was I supposed to do? Ignore him?"

"Yes!" said William, nearly jumping out of his seat. "Yes, *got*dammit! But oh no. Not your ass. You made it look as if we weren't on the same page."

"We weren't," said Janet.

"That wasn't his business," said Kimmie.

142

"You made it his business."

"He asked a question and I answered it," Janet said. "That's all I did. And I never once heard him say you weren't getting the contract."

"He didn't have to say it. His silence spoke volumes. You're the only one who doesn't seem to understand that."

"You shouldn't have brought her along," said Kimmie. "I told you that when you were saying you wanted her to be involved in more higher profile cases. I told you that's not a good idea. I told you that just last night." And then she caught herself. "This morning," she said.

Janet remained quiet. She answered a question. That was all she did. How could that be wrong? They didn't give her credit for anything! But that was all the more reason why she felt good about her decision.

And when they made it back to the office, she didn't delay. She went to her cubicle, pulled the letter up on her computer, changed the date, printed it out, and walked over to Kimmie's office.

"What's this?" Kimmie asked when Janet handed the letter to her.

"It's my resignation," Janet said. "I'm giving two weeks' notice."

Kimmie looked at the paper, and then looked at Janet. "Resignation? You can't resign! We've got the end-of-year markups to submit. You always do that for our unit, Jane."

"I showed you how to do it numerous times," Janet said.

"But I couldn't understand that shit! And you know it! You can't resign!"

"I'm resigning, Kimmie. It's not up for debate."

Kimmie couldn't believe it. "Then you're the one's going to tell him," she said, hurrying from behind her desk. "Come with me!"

She marched Janet down the hall to William Rice's office. One knock on his door and she entered without waiting for permission. Janet entered behind her.

"I'm busy," William said.

Kimmie placed the resignation letter on William's desk. He didn't bother to pick it up. "What's this?"

Kimmie looked at Janet.

"It's my resignation," Janet said.

William frowned. "Resignation? You're going to resign after what you did to me in Tulsa? You'd better be grateful I didn't fire your ass!"

"I'm resigning," said Janet. She wasn't about to have a firing on her resume. "I'm giving two-weeks' notice."

"Two weeks my ass," William said.

"You're getting off my premises now. Get out now!"

Janet was angry too. "Put it in writing."

William frowned. So did Kimmie. "What?" Kimmie asked.

"I offered two weeks' notice in my resignation letter. You will not put on my record that I abandoned my position when I don't show up for work for the next two weeks. Put it in writing that you want me out today, and I'll be happy to leave right now."

William was livid. "You don't tell me what to do you . . . you . . ."

All three of them knew what he wanted to say. But he didn't have the nerve to say it.

"Just get out," he said. "Get out now!"

"Then I need to remove that two weeks' clause out of my letter," Janet said.

Kimmie looked at William. He nodded his head. And Kimmie pulled out a pad, wrote that Janet was asked to leave today rather than the two weeks' standard as per her resignation letter, and then Janet accepted the signed and dated page.

She had been applying everywhere, ever since she knew she'd never get ahead, nor get any respect at Rooney and Rice. She had hoped to have a position lined up before she submitted her resignation. That was why she was holding it back. She already was living paycheck to paycheck as it was. But she followed her instincts. And her instincts had told her that today necessitated that she resign before they fired her. Three weeks before Christmas.

She told Beth and Marveen goodbye, and a few others in the office, but Kimmie was watching and none of them wanted to be on her shit list. They barely grunted in Janet's direction. People who couldn't stop running to her for her help, suddenly didn't know her name. Suddenly didn't want to know her name. So Janet just grabbed up the few items she owned, and left.

It felt like the time when she left the Henleys.

Only this time there was nothing to celebrate.

Only this time it didn't feel like freedom.

It felt like failure.

CHAPTER SIXTEEN

He leaned back on the sofa, inside the video room of his home in Tulsa, and pressed the button on the remote control. With his legs crossed, a pad and pen in his hand, his reading glasses on, and a lit cigar between his fingers, he looked at the 90-inch monitor as the recordings of his daily meetings appeared on screen. Because he recorded all of his daily briefings and meetings, too, each had been labeled by his assistant and stored according to meeting time. But the only one he was interested in seeing again was the first one. A meeting he had held with a conglomerate from Rome looking to invest in Shetfield Oil. Richard had nothing to do with that aspect of the Shetfield empire. He rarely even ventured into the state of Texas where their largest refinery was housed. But he had promised his older brother to take the meeting and give his recommendations. Richard knew next to nothing about oil, but he was spot on about human behavior. His brother needed to know if those businessmen were looking for an amicable partnership, or a hostile takeover, something his brother constantly had to deal with.

He took some notes as he watched and listened to those men in the meeting. His first impression had been a negative one, but he couldn't put his finger on why. That was why he recorded every meeting. To go back and find out why. And as he watched and listened, he got his answer. And took down notes.

He was still writing when the video of that meeting ended, and the video of the second meeting he held that day came on. The meeting with the representatives of Rooney and Rice. When he heard the comment, "now this is what I call a room," he looked up. And that was when he realized the next meeting was being shown. He almost looked back down. That meeting, in his view, was a colossal waste of time. Rooney and Rice might be a big deal in Cope, but they weren't ready for prime time in his world. But just as he was looking back down at his writing pad, the camera caught a whiff of *her*, and he looked back up.

Janet.

Janet Evans.

But they called her Jane at Rooney and Rice.

He remembered holding her all night that night as if it had happened yesterday. He remembered how he'd never laid in a bed with a woman before without having sex with her, but how he'd never been more satisfied in his life.

He remembered that next morning, too. And how he still hadn't gotten over that one. How he still felt as if he had ruined her life. Was she married now? Did she have kids? He never checked on her. He felt, had he found out, he would not have been man enough to leave her alone. He didn't have some man look into it for him, nor did he check himself. He manned-up, and left her alone.

He took a slow drag on his cigar as he watched to see her face in the group. When she was too far away for him to render any conclusions, he grabbed the remote and isolated her in the frame. And he magnified her. Now she was as large as his monitor screen.

And that was when he saw it again. That something that had pricked him when he laid eyes on her again at that meeting. That something he thereafter tried to ignore, but he kept taking peeps at her because it was too strong to ignore.

But what was it that he was seeing? She had such a strong face. A face that had been hewn from a rock of offense, in Richard's view, where soft beds and sweet childhoods had not been a part of her past. She'd seen a lot. She'd been through a lot. And the trauma of that hard life she wore like a second skin all over her face. Even as her skin, he'd also noticed, was smoother than any he'd ever recalled. Even as her hazel eyes appeared as witnesses to the harshness of the world, but still managed to retain their softness, and sweetness, and, he would daresay, innocence.

Wow, he thought as he stared at her. As he froze the frame, with a picture of her larger than life, on his massive screen. And it suddenly flooded back to him. He should have given it a shot. He might have actually been happy in this life, had he given her a chance.

She was the girl from Grundy Street. She was the girl with the innocent eyes. She was the girl he'd wished to God, for years on end, that he had never left that morning. But not for her sake. For his sake.

He looked down, at her small hands. There was no ring on it. None. Which should not have made him feel some kind of way, but it did. He felt a sense of what? Relief? Thrill that she might still be available? But that was craziness on top of craziness!

"Janet," he said out loud, staring at her. "Janet Evans."

"And who exactly is Janet Evans?"

Richard almost jumped out of his skin when he heard a voice just above his head. He turned quickly. And it was only then, when he saw that it was his big brother standing just behind him, did he settle back down. "You almost scared the shit out of me, Monty!" he angrily protested.

Montgomery "Monty" Shetfield smiled. "Almost?" he responded in his usual deadpan way.

"How do you do that?" Richard asked. "A mouse makes more noise than your big ass when they break into somebody's house. Which is what you just did, by the way. Your big ass just broke in here without permission. How did you do it? And take off that big-ass hat in my home!"

"Make me," Monty said without the theatrics of his brother as he walked around and sat in one of the two wing chairs flanking the sofa. Richard was right. He was a big man. Whereas Richard was six feet tall, Monty was six-three and even more muscular than Richard. And he stretched out every inch of that tall muscularity when he sat down.

And he didn't remove his giant, Texas-size hat either.

"I ask again," Monty said. "Who's Janet

Evans?"

Richard gave his brother a hard look. Everybody thought he ran the Shetfield empire because he was so glitzy and was always out front. But he didn't. He ran his own empire. Monty ran Shetfield Oil, which eclipsed anything else in their portfolio.

Monty looked at him. "Who is she?"

Richard finally looked away from his brother and at the screen again. At Janet's life size face on that screen. "She works for Rooney and Rice."

"For who and who?"

"A consulting firm," Richard said, staring at her again, as took another drag on his cigar.

"I thought Trevor Reese handled our consulting," Monty said.

"He does."

"Then why are you," Monty started to say. And then he caught himself. "Let me guess," he said. "She interests you?"

But Richard didn't respond. He twirled the butt of his cigar around in his mouth and continued to stare at the screen.

Monty stared, too, and ultimately hunched his shoulders. "I don't get it," he said. "She's not your usual cup of tea at all."

"Didn't know I had a cup of tea," Richard shot back.

"Oh, you have one. Big hair. Big boobs. Big ass. Or should I say, in the case of your women, fake hair, fake boobs, fake ass."

"There's nothing wrong with enhancements," Richard said. "It's a woman's prerogative."

"I prefer the natural look."

"In Texas? The capital of fake? Give me a break! Besides," Richard added, still staring at Janet, "it doesn't get any more natural than Miss Evans. She's not even wearing makeup."

Monty stared at Janet on that big screen, and then he looked at his brother. "Leave her alone, Dick. She's out of your league."

Richard smiled. "Really?"

"Yes, really!"

"And how do you suppose that?"

"Because she looks like she's ethical and has some pride about herself. She's not one of your money-grubbing sluts. But you dangle something as powerful as all your attributes in somebody's face, they'll become as slutty as they need to be. Don't turn her out like that. When you love and leave those women of yours, the money you give them soothes their hurt. You love and leave a girl like her? Money won't soothe shit with her. You'll devastate her. Leave her alone, Dick."

Richard continued to stare at that face on

the screen. His brother had a point, although he was wrong about one thing. Richard never loved and left any woman. Because he never loved any woman. And his ladies understood that he never would. Whenever he left them, and he always did, they had nothing to cry about because he never pretended it was anything more than what it was. But had he tried, he just might have made something happen with somebody like Janet. He might not have left her.

But he'd never know now.

But he did know loneliness was like a heavy load in his life. And he was getting tired of carrying it.

"How did the meeting go with the Italians?" Monty asked.

Richard finally looked away from Janet. "It went."

"Are they looking for a partner, or a takeover?"

"They want to get in, learn everything they can about the oil industry from the top of the line, and then compete against us. They couldn't manage a takeover bid. They don't have the muscle for that, given who you are. But they want to compete on the same stage as you. And they want you to show them how."

"Your verdict?"

"I wouldn't trust them. There's such a thing as good competition. They'll be dangerous competition."

Monty nodded. "I came down the same way," he said. "What do you suppose we do about it? We might turn them down, but that doesn't mean they won't become dangerous competition in the near future. What can we do about it?"

"We? We can do nothing about it. Me? I'm going to have a meeting with them. Offer them a backdoor deal. See which way they bite. Then we'll know where they're coming from."

"And then?"

"And then we come at them the same way. Take'em for everything they've got. Use them as the example of what happens to fools who mess with us."

Monty smiled. "Ruthless Richard. You live up to your name."

Richard didn't respond to that. "I just do it to them before they do it to us."

Monty stood on his feet. "Good. Just let me know if you need backup."

"Ha! You? The Texan? You Texans are big talkers. I don't need conversation."

"Then you shall not get any. Bye, brother," he said as he started to leave.

Richard looked up at him. "That's it?

Pick my brain and go?"

"Don't forget I criticized you too," Monty said with a smile that could charm birds from trees.

Richard smiled, too, although his smile looked unnatural on his stern face. "Just remember to re-alarm my home as you leave. How it didn't trigger is a mystery to me."

"I'll see you next Saturday," Monty said as he began heading toward the exit.

Richard frowned. "What's going on next Saturday?"

"Dad's wife's birthday. It's always a week before Christmas."

"They haven't divorced yet?" Richard asked.

"If you were around more you would know the answer to that question," said Monty. "No, they haven't divorced yet. Just get your ass to Texas next Saturday."

"I can't stand his new wife. Why would I bother?"

"Because none of Pop's friends are going to show. They took Mom's side when Dad divorced her. That's why he needs all of us there. His mail order bride doesn't know anybody in the States at all. If we don't show, it'll just be him and her."

"And they deserve everything they're

getting," Richard said. "Cheated on Ma all those years and then he divorces her? And for some tramp like that?"

"Have you even spoken to Ma since you got back in the States?"

"I just got back last night," Richard said.

"Ma has moved on," Monty said. "You need to move on too."

Richard exhaled. He was a man in his thirties, but he still felt the sting of his parents' divorce. And his father's sudden and unexpected marriage to some Russian bombshell he barely knew. She wasn't a mail order bride the way he and Monty referred to her as, but it was close enough for them. "I'll be there," he said. "But only to drop by. Then I'll spend the rest of my time with Mom."

"Suit yourself," Monty said, leaving. "Just show up."

"And don't break in my house ever again!"

"I love you too," Monty said back to him without turning around. Richard gave him another unnatural smile and watched until he was clean out of sight.

And then he turned his attention back to Janet.

And he was staring at her again. And twirling the butt of his cigar in his mouth again.

Monty was right. He should leave her alone. She was just too different than any woman he was used to being with. But all those women he had ever been with weren't suitable for anything but bed action. And his body was getting tired of just that. He needed more. His perspective had changed. He needed to stretch his horizons. He needed to find out, once and for all, if a woman like Miss Evans held the key that could unlock his heart. Was that what was drawing him to her when they first met? Is that what kept her on his mind all these years later? Or would she be the one to lock up his heart even tighter than it already was, and throw away the key?

Maybe, all these years, he hadn't been afraid of hurting her. He knew now that he wouldn't hurt her if he decided to go down that road with her. Maybe, all these years, he had been afraid of her hurting him.

But was it too late? Did she hate him now? Did she even remember him?

Nothing beats a failure but a try.

What the hell did he have to lose?

He picked up the phone quickly, before he changed his mind.

CHAPTER SEVENTEEN

Keeping pace with Mo Riley was nearly impossible, but Janet managed somehow. They had been walking for several minutes. Nearly two miles by her calculation. And it didn't look as if he was trying to slow down. But by the time they made it to the park, she had to put her foot down.

"You're killing me, Mo," she said, barely able to catch her breath.

When he looked back, she was sitting on the park bench. He smiled and shook his head. And walked back to her. "I was nearly dead in that nursing home when you found me. Now look at me. A specimen of health!"

"Yes, you are."

"And look at you. Nearly dead."

Janet laughed. "Keep bragging, old man. I can always return you where I found you."

"Not possible. I can outrun you now."

Janet laughed again. "So true!" she said.

Mo continued to stare at her. And then he sat down too. "You gon tell me what's going on?" he asked her.

"Meaning?" she asked him.

"You came home early from work yesterday. Didn't say a word to me, so I didn't say a word to you. I figure you had to get your thoughts together. But now it's a new day and you still haven't told me anything, Baby Girl."

She hadn't told him because she was still getting over it herself. Six years on a job she actually enjoyed doing, and one she did well, and it came down to this? Resign before they fire you? She looked at him. "What do you want to know?"

"Why you ain't at work?" Mo asked her.

Janet exhaled. It still felt strange to her too. "I resigned," she said.

Mo frowned. "Why would you do a fool thing like that? You got another job lined up?"

Another disappointment. "Nothing's come through yet," she said. "But I've applied everywhere."

But Mo was disturbed. "Wait a minute here," he said. "You done quit your job, and you ain't got no job lined up? I raised you better than that, the couple of years I did raise you, Janet. Those Horrible Henleys teach you that foolishness? You don't quit no job without no job!"

"It was the spur of the moment. I didn't plan to submit my resignation until another job came through for me. But I couldn't stay there."

"Why the hell not?"

"Because I couldn't, Mo! They treated me like I was a doormat. New people walk through the door, I train them, and then they're walking over me too. At some point you get tired of that. It took me six long years. But I'm tired of it now."

"But you don't have another job."

Janet's face showed her anxiety. "No, I don't.

"Don't let anybody run you off your job, Baby Girl," Mo said. "You hear me? Jobs are too hard to find in this economy. And especially for a black girl in Cope. They barely want us to have anything as it is. And you done up and quit a good office job like that?"

"They haven't given me a raise in five years, Mo. Every time I ask, they say the budget won't allow it. But every time a new person comes along, I have to train them and the budget manages to find a way to give them what they're worth. And they all got one thing in common."

"They white," Mo said.

"Nope. Black women come up in there, too, and advance over me. But they're all beauty queens. Every one of them. That's the commonality. William Rice seems to think a public relations firm needs to project a certain image."

"And that image ain't you?" Mo asked.

"Apparently not," Janet said with a tinge

of sadness wrapped with bitterness in her voice.

Mo stared at her. He was from a generation and culture that didn't go around resigning from jobs just because they didn't treat you right. They expected not to be treated right. That was never a surprise.

But Janet deserved better. She suffered long enough. And he knew it. "You did the right thing," he said to her.

She looked at him. She never expected him to understand.

"I don't have none of that book smarts like you got," Mo said, "but I got street smarts in abundance. And on the street where I come from, we would say you didn't give up. You gave in. And there's a difference. Sometimes it makes more sense to stop beating your head against a rock, and just walk away. You did the right thing, Baby Girl."

Janet nodded. It was good to know that he was still in her corner. But it hurt too. Because she didn't have another job. Because she just walked away from a job she enjoyed doing. Tears appeared in her big hazel eyes.

When Mo saw her tears, he was outdone. "Come here, child," he said to her. And she slid over on the bench and leaned into his arms.

And they stayed that way for several minutes. Until Janet was able to wipe all her tears away, and sit back up on her own. "I'm okay," she reassured him. "Don't worry about me."

"I have to worry about you. If I don't, who will?"

Janet smiled. That was the truth. Mo was all she had.

But Mo wasn't smiling. "Are we in trouble?" he asked her.

She quickly shook her head. "We can manage for now. I have enough savings to tie us over for a little bit."

"And my social security check," said Mo.

But Janet was already shaking her head. "No, Mo," she said. "You only get seven-hundred-and-sixty-dollars a month. That's your fun money, and it's gonna stay that way."

"I've been living off you long enough. It's time I carry my weight around here."

Janet's cell phone began ringing. "You've never lived off of anybody in your life before. Don't even try that!" Then she exhaled. "With the help of the Lord, we're be okay," she said to him.

"I hope the Lord's listening," he said to her.

"He always is," she said to him as she looked at her Caller ID. When she saw that it was from Shetfield, Incorporated, she was puzzled. Was it Richard? She quickly answered it. "Hello?"

"May I speak with Miss Evans?"

"This is she."

"Miss Evans, this is Doris Wilson. We met on yesterday."

"Yes, I remember."

"Mr. Shetfield will see you tomorrow evening at eight thirty. Please take down the address."

"Oh, no, Ms. Wilson. There's been some mistake. I'm no longer employed with Rooney and Rice."

Mo looked at her.

"Take down the address, please."

"But ma'am, you aren't hearing me. I was there in my capacity as an employee of Rooney and Rice Consulting firm. I am no longer in their employ. There's been some mistake."

"There's been no mistake. Take down the address. And be there tomorrow at eight thirty sharp."

Janet was utterly confused. Why would Richard Shetfield want to meet with her, and to meet with her at eight thirty at night? It made no sense!

But he was rich. And rich people, she knew, did whatever they liked.

She took down the address.

When she ended the call, she still looked puzzled.

"What was that about?" Mo asked her.

"Richard Shetfield wants to meet with me tomorrow night," she said.

Mo frowned. "Not *that* Shetfield?"

Janet nodded. "That Shetfield," she said.

"You applied to work for the Shetfields?"

"No! 'Course not. I went to a meeting with Mr. Rice and Kimmie yesterday at Shetfield's office. But we left with the impression he wasn't going to hire the firm."

"Then why he wanna meet with you?"

Janet shook her head. "I have no idea, Mo." She had some idea. But she was sure it wasn't *that*.

Mo exhaled. "Be careful, Baby Girl. All I can tell you. You may not wanna work for that crew. Those Shetfields will chew you up and spit you out. And then put you under their shoe and squash you like a bug. Be careful," he said again.

But Janet already knew that.

CHAPTER EIGHTEEN

"They must take us for fools."

Spencer Shetfield, Richard's kid brother, drove his classic 1967 Mustang Fastback up to the empty strip mall and stopped at the curb in front of what was soon to be a jewelry store. "Setting up a meeting with a man of your esteem in an area like this. There's nothing out here!"

"They plan to revitalize this whole side of town," Richard said as he sat on the passenger side unbuckling his seatbelt. "They plan to build this mall first, and then build a community around it."

Spencer unbuckled his seatbelt too. "Sounds like some ass-backwards shit to me. Bring the people first, I say, then the businesses will follow."

"I say bring them both at the same time," Richard said as he got out of the Mustang. "But what do I know about business?"

Spencer laughed, grabbed his sunglasses off the dashboard even though it was cold outside and no sun in sight, and he got out too. He was the family's trust fund baby.

Everybody worked, but him. He started looking around. "I don't know, Dick," he said. "I don't like the backdrop."

"I had my guys check'em out," said Richard. "They didn't find anything to worry about."

"Yeah but, Dick," said Spencer, looking at his brother as if he should know better.

"*Yea but Dick* what?" asked Richard.

"They're Italians!" Spencer said.

"Now-now, Spence," Richard said. "That sounds racist to me. How would you like it if somebody said, 'yeah, but they're Irish!'" The Shetfield family tree took root in Ireland.

But Spencer started shaking his head and grinning that charming grin everybody loved. "I would say damn right, they are. Watch your back!"

Richard laughed. Spencer was incorrigible! And honest as hell. That was why he trusted him above any in their family. And like all of the Shetfields, Spencer knew how to handle himself around thugs as well as kings.

Then Spencer looked at his big brother, who was five years older than he was, and put on his sunglasses. "I asked her you know," he said.

Richard looked at him. "When?"

"Last night."

"She said yes?"

"I know you didn't ask me that! What else was she going to say? No lady is going to turn me down!"

Richard ignored that and stared at him. "And you're serious about this?"

"You know I'm serious. I wouldn't have asked her if I wasn't."

But Spencer kept looking at Richard. "What about you?" he asked him.

Richard knew where that conversation was going. He looked away from Spencer at the empty highway across the parking lot. They were truly in the middle of nowhere. "What about me?"

"You aren't getting any younger, Dicky. Playing the field is cute when you're young. It's pathetic when you're old."

Richard smiled. "You sound more and more like Monty every day."

Spencer was offended. "Don't you tell that lie! Me like that stiff-shirt? Never on this earth!"

Richard laughed.

"But I'm serious, Dicky. You aren't getting any younger."

"Don't worry about me," Richard said. "I'll never grow old."

But Spencer failed to see the humor.

"That's what Michael Jackson said," he said. "Better watch yourself."

Richard frowned. "*What*?"

"Michael Jackson said he was Peter Pan and he would never grow old. He was right. He died when he was fifty. Don't talk to me about never growing old. Don't put that shit out in the universe like that. You most definitely want to grow old!"

"Okay, alright," said Richard, surprised by Spencer's distress. "I take it back."

"And," Spencer said, "you most definitely do not want to grow old alone," he added, and looked at Richard.

Richard stared at him. Then he exhaled. "I'm having dinner with Janet tomorrow night," he said.

Spencer frowned. "Janet? Who's Janet?" Then he realized who. And Spencer was shocked. He was the only person, six years ago, that Richard had ever mentioned her to. "But I thought you said you were going to leave her alone. I thought you said she was too good for you and you weren't going to hurt her like that."

"I'm not going to hurt her. I'm going to have dinner with her," Richard said.

But Spencer was still suspicious. "To what end?" he asked him.

"I'm not going to hurt her, alright?"

"She's a sista," Spencer said. "And you know how Monty is about the sistas. You'd better not hurt her. He'll come looking for you."

Richard looked at Spencer. Everybody knew that their oldest brother Monty didn't date anybody but black women. But he'd never known Monty to be protective of any of them. "What are you talking about?" Richard asked Spencer. "Monty never had a problem when I slept with all those other black women and dumped them. Why would he care what happens to Janet?"

"Because those black hoes you date are just like your white hoes. Just as long as you give them a wonderful parting gift, as you always do, you could dump them every day of the week. They don't give a damn about your butt either. But Janet is different."

Spencer had never met Janet Evans, but he'd heard about her. Richard told him how she was still a virgin at twenty-two, which shocked Spencer. A twenty-two-year-old virgin was like a unicorn where they came from. And although Richard never told him so, he was certain she wasn't a twenty-two-year-old virgin anymore when his brother got through with her. That was probably why he bought her that Mercedes.

But the shock to Spencer was when she

returned that Mercedes. She became a folk hero to Spencer when she pulled gangster shit like that on his brother. That played with his brother's mind for a long time. He'd never seen a woman like Janet. Neither had Spencer.

"What's your motive, is the question," Spencer said.

"Dinner is my motive," said Richard.

"And?"

"None of your business."

"Then why did you bring it up?"

Richard frowned. "I don't know."

"Did it have something to do with the fact that I'm younger than you and looking to hitch my wagon, while your old ass don't have a wagon to hitch?"

"I don't know," Richard answered honestly.

"You think she's the one?" Spencer asked.

"No!" Richard said. Then he settled back down. "I don't know," he said.

Spencer shook his head. "You don't know shit, do you?"

Richard smiled and pushed his brother aside. Then he looked beyond his brother. "There they are," he said, and then he and Spencer watched a car turn off the empty highway and drive through the big parking lot, kicking up dust, toward Spencer's Mustang.

"How many are we looking at?" Spencer asked, walking around to the passenger side of his vehicle.

Richard was trying to see inside of the tinted car. "The driver," he said. "A guy in the back too. A passenger. Three. I see three guys."

"Three guys?" Spencer nodded his head. "And it's just two of us."

"We can handle three guys all day long," Richard said. "That used to be my M-O at every frat party on campus. Me against a group of guys. And I always won."

Spencer looked at his brother. "College? You do realize that was damn-near twenty years ago when you were in college, right?"

"Twenty years? That long? Damn!" Richard said, playing around, and Spencer laughed too.

And then the Italians stopped beside the Mustang and stepped out.

Richard and Spencer leaned against the Mustang and the three Italians leaned against their Cadillac. "Who is that?" the one in the middle, Bartoli, asked.

"This is my brother Spencer," Richard said. "Spence, this is Bartoli and?"

"Scapaletti and Vance," said Bartoli. "I

thought we were meeting you alone," he added.

"I thought I was meeting you alone," said Richard.

Bartoli smiled. "Touché," he said.

"Interesting location for a meeting place," Richard said, his arms folded, his legs crossed at the ankle.

"Just wanted to show you what a partnership with us could lead to," Bartoli said.

Spencer knew he was joking. "To a strip mall?" he asked. "You're pulling our leg, right?"

Richard could tell Bartoli didn't think he was. Richard could tell Bartoli thought owning a strip mall in the middle of nowhere was quite the feat.

"You do realize who we are, right?" Spencer asked. "You do realize strip malls don't mean shit to us, right?"

The other two Italians glanced at their boss.

"I understand you're an asshole, if that's what you mean," Bartoli said to Spencer and Spencer was about to rush him. But Richard pulled him back.

"No need for that," Richard said, slamming his younger brother against the car.

"Why did you want to meet, Mr. Shetfield?" Bartoli asked. "We met already and you didn't seem impressed then."

"I was impressed," Richard said, "but I knew my brother wouldn't be."

"Why wouldn't he be?" Bartoli asked.

"He has an aversion to crooks," Richard said. "He doesn't get in the mud with thugs."

Bartoli's men were offended again. But Bartoli stared at Richard. "If we're such crooks and thugs," he asked, "why are you here? Why did you ask to meet?"

"I want to give you an offer you can't refuse," said Richard, and Spencer smiled.

"What kind of offer?" Bartoli asked.

"A backdoor into Shetfield Oil," said Richard.

"But you just said your brother--"

"Not through Monty," Richard said. "Through me."

Bartoli stared at him. "You don't run Shetfield Oil. Your brother does."

"But my brother and I, this brother right here, are stakeholders. Major stakeholders. If we combine our shares, we can overrule our brother."

That was the first Spencer was hearing of any takeover attempt, but he knew how to play it off. There was always method to Richard's madness.

But Bartoli wasn't playing it off. "Who do you think you're fucking with?" he asked. "We did our research. Montgomery is your father's favorite. Without question. Your father will side with your brother Monty, and between the two of them and all of their shares, you two won't stand a chance."

"Our mother is a stakeholder too," said Richard. "And guess who's her favorite?"

Spencer started to ask who because Richard wasn't close to either parent. He wasn't close to anybody but Spence and Monty.

But it was enough to maintain Bartoli's interest. "What are you saying?"

"I'm saying I've been looking at a takeover for some time now," Richard said. "I just needed the right muscle on my side."

"Muscle? We're businesspeople. Do we look like muscle to you?"

"Like you stepped out of a muscle magazine," said Spencer.

Bartoli frowned. "I don't like you," he said to Spencer.

"Good," said Spencer. "That only redounds to my good character if a character like you loathes me. And it's mutual, by the way."

"You want in or not?" Richard asked Bartoli.

"What's in it for me?" asked Bartoli.

"If it works. And that's a big if. But if it

works," Richard said, "three percent of Shetfield Oil, which would be huge. You were only asking Monty for two."

Bartoli was interested. Richard could tell he and his boys were interested. "Keep talking," Bartoli said.

"No more talking," Richard shot back. "I need you to decide. Are you in, or are you out?"

Bartoli smiled. "I'm in," he said. "It's what I wanted all along."

"A takeover?"

"That's right. But I had to get inside first. I knew that too."

And just like that, Richard's relaxed demeanor left. "I thought so, motherfucker!" he said angrily.

Even Spencer was surprised how quickly Richard's demeanor changed. "What are you talking?"

"You think I'll stand by and let you take over my family business? Are you out of your fucking mind?"

Bartoli panicked. "You're the one who brought up takeover!" he declared.

"Because I knew what your ass really wanted. Now get out of my face with that bullshit!"

Bartoli and his men were piping mad. Spencer wondered if their heads were going to explode. But they knew they had no choice but to walk away. They knew they weren't in any condition to start a war with a Shetfield.

"You'll regret this," Bartoli warned. "You don't know who you're fucking with." But he also got in that car, and the three Italians sped away.

Spencer smiled. "I knew your ass wasn't stupid enough to go against Monty."

"Let's get out of here," Richard said as he got in on the passenger side and Spencer, still smiling, got in behind the wheel.

But then, just as he was about to start his ignition, Bartoli's car suddenly turned around at the end of the parking lot and began racing back toward the Mustang.

Spencer, seeing it too, was about to crank up. But Richard stopped him. "Stay where you are," he said, looking through his side mirror at the fast-approaching car. "We've got this. I'll take Bartoli and the guy in the backseat. You take the driver."

"Sure we got this, Dicky?" Spencer asked as he stared through the rearview and pulled out his loaded revolver.

"I'm never sure," Richard said, pulling out his gun too. "But that never stopped me before."

And as soon as the three Italians jumped out of that car with guns in hand, and began running toward the Shetfields, Richard and

Spencer jumped out of the Mustang. And before the Italians could raise their guns to aim it at the brothers, the brothers were already shooting. Richard took out Bartoli and the backseat passenger, and Spencer quickly dispensed with the driver. It was a fast take-out, but it was still pulse-pounding to the brothers.

But Bartoli was down, but not out. He turned onto his back and tried to fire a shot at Richard. But Richard had not let down his guard yet. And he took him out.

Then both brothers looked at each other. "What the fuck, Dicky?" a shocked Spencer said. "Did you see that shit?"

"I saw it."

"You saw this coming?"

Richard exhaled. He was reeling, too, because he saw no such thing. But he wasn't telling Spencer that. "I see everything coming," he said.

CHAPTER NINETEEN

She arrived at the address given, which turned out to be a high-end restaurant on the outskirts of Tulsa. But as she waited to drive up to the valet station, her Honda Civic looking conspicuously odd with the luxury cars that surrounded her, she couldn't help but wonder why he would need to meet with her at a restaurant, rather than his office? And what if she went through all that trouble of getting dressed, and driving the distance, only to find out that he didn't realize she was no longer with Rooney and Rice? His secretary indicated that she knew, but what if she failed to mention it to him? But the bigger question for Janet, was why did she agree to come at all? All she had to say was no.

But she didn't say no. She agreed to show up. Part of it was just the curiosity of why he wanted to meet with her. But the other part of it was that it was Richard who wanted to meet with her. The man who didn't mind having dinner with her in her poverty-stricken boarding room. The man who held her all night to help ease her recurring nightmare. The man who was so concerned about her walking in the dark that he purchased her a car that would have had no problem fitting in among the luxury cars around her now. She was excited to see Richard again.

Although, she also knew, he was the man who made love to her, and left her.

Although, she also knew, if that meeting two days ago was any indication, he didn't even remember her.

And why would he? Her life was no movie of the week. She wasn't going to suddenly get some exotic makeover and become the Cinderella of the ball that every man wanted to be with. Including a man like Richard. It was nonsensical to even think it!

But she couldn't back out now. She was already there, in line, and the valet was motioning her to pull her car forward. She pulled up, got out, took her valet ticket, and handed off her keys. And then she slowly entered the restaurant praying it would amount to something positive, but careful to assume that it wouldn't.

Richard was already inside. Seated at his booth, he was leaned back, sipping wine, and taking puffs on his well-smoked cigar. And still reeling from that interaction with those Italians. They were angry because he was on to them and they apparently decided, right then and there, to take him and his kid brother out. And he didn't see it coming, despite what he told Spence. And it worried him that he didn't.

And then his focus shifted, when Janet walked in.

He had a ringside seat as he watched her. She had a proud constitution about her, he thought, as she stood in line in the popular restaurant and waited her turn at the Maître d station. She had the look of somebody who wasn't trying to be about any nonsense and was only there to handle her business. Stern might be the word some would describe her. Serious was how he saw her.

And her dress style, he also realized, pleased him too. Because it was so very understated. Because nothing about her was overdone. She wore a gorgeous blue dress that hugged every curve of her slender frame, and that brought out the brilliance of her big, beautiful hazel eyes, but it wasn't dripping with lavish jewels or extravagant lacings, as was the style of choice for most women in that restaurant. Her hair was also nicely done, dropping just past her neckline in large curls that framed her interesting face. And her jewelry only consisted of a pair of small earrings, and a string of pearls at the throat. She looked quite elegant, Richard thought.

But so different too! Because all he'd ever been interested in was a certain kind of woman with a certain kind of look. Although they ranged in ethnicity, from white to black to Asian to Hispanic to all other races in between, and in size, from skinny girls with model-type bodies to voluptuous women on the verge of plumpness, they all had one thing in common: gorgeous faces. Faces to die for.

Janet didn't have that attribute, if he were to be honest. Her face was more interesting than drop-dead gorgeous, and he never thought in a million years that interesting could ever trump gorgeous. But somehow, on Janet, it did.

Whenever he looked at Janet, it seemed as if he was looking at a woman who made gorgeousness seem plain. Who made gorgeous women seem like a dime a dozen. Because in every room, you could pick out a dozen of them. But just one of Janet.

But the fact remained: he'd never known a girl like her. And he still couldn't verbalize to his own satisfaction why he phoned Doris and told her to contact Janet at all. Why would he put her on this bridge to nowhere? Why would he put himself on it? She was so not his type. What was he doing?

But she was there now. He had done the damn thing and had his secretary ask her to come there. He might as well see where it led.

He smashed his cigar in the ashtray on his table and stood to his feet as the maître d led her to his booth.

When Janet saw him stand up buttoning his suitcoat, she smiled and began extending her hand well before she made it all the way up to him. As if she was meeting a client, not the man of her dreams. It was her way to manage her nerves.

But as soon as she got close enough to his booth, and he shook her hand, he knew that wasn't enough. Because it all flooded back to him. There was something about Janet that made him feel warm inside. That was so indescribable that it would do her an injustice to put her in any category. She did something to him. That was all there was to it. And he removed his hand from hers, and pulled her into his arms.

Janet was surprised when he hugged her. No man had ever hugged her before or since Richard did six years ago. Now he was doing it again. And she couldn't help herself. She loved that feeling! She even closed her eyes tightly to experience every moment of that feeling. She felt his big hands on her small back. She felt his hard body against her soft body. She smelled his cologne scent mixed with the scent of cigar. Nobody made her experience feelings the way Richard did.

Richard couldn't help it either. He closed his eyes too. He was a drowning man. Nobody would believe it to look at him and his accomplishments, but if something didn't change in his life, he was going down for the count. What Janet's presence did was to give him hope. She made him feel that it wasn't all hopeless. That he could actually do right by a female for once in his life. That love and happiness wasn't some foreign concept that wasn't meant for him. He held Janet so tightly, with her breasts crushed against his chest, and he didn't want to let her go.

It was Janet who pulled back from him. Because this was crazy! Because she had to know that man was just being polite, and for her to give it any more significance than that would be foolhardy. For all she knew he greeted everybody that way. A strange way to greet everybody, she realized, but the rich did things differently. Maybe Richard was a hugger. He didn't give her that impression when she saw him two days ago. But what else could be the reason?

Richard was a little embarrassed that he had overreacted on seeing her, and he tried to play it off by being all about the business too.

"Have a seat," he said to her.

Neither one of them had realized it, but the maître d was still waiting. "What would the lady care to drink, sir?" he asked Richard.

And Richard took that opportunity to lash out at the maître d. To make it all about that poor man, rather than Richard's own embarrassment. "Why are you asking me what she care to drink? Ask the lady!"

"I apologize, ma'am."

"No apology needed," Janet said politely. "I'll have a vodka?"

"Very good, ma'am," the maître d said, and left their table.

Richard sat down. "I was rude, wasn't I?" he said to her.

"Very," Janet said. "I'm sure that man didn't mean anything by it. He was just kowtowing to the person with the power."

"Don't excuse that," Richard shot back at her. "Demand to be seen, even when people don't want to see you. You understand?"

"Oh, I do. And I have. All my life."

"But?"

"But there's so much of that in my world that you have to pick your battles. And an insensitive waiter isn't a battle I have the energy to fight. His insensitivity doesn't matter to me enough," she said with a smile.

Richard smiled too. "Point taken," he said. Then he exhaled, and glanced down at her breasts. "It's good seeing you again, Janet," he said.

Janet stared at him. "You mean from two days ago?"

"I mean from six years ago."

Janet smiled. "You remember me?"

Richard frowned. "I absolutely remember you. I never forgot you."

Janet was shocked to hear it. She'd never forgotten him, either, but she chalked that up to her own desperate need. But there was nothing desperate about Richard, and he never forgot her! Now she was intrigued.

"What have you been doing with yourself?" he asked her.

"Working. Living. Doing what people do with themselves."

Richard laughed. "Got cha," he said. "Although," he added, "you're no longer with Rooney and Rice. Why not?"

Janet exhaled. "It goes back to fighting battles. That's all I've been doing for six years at that firm and it got me nowhere."

"So, you gave up?"

"I gave in. Especially after our meeting with you."

"With me? Why would that little meeting

cause you to give in?"

"Mr. Rice seemed to think I was the reason he lost that contract."

"Nonsense! He never had the contract to lose," Richard said.

"But he decided to make it all about me. And I was tired of every negative turn being all about me. I already planned to leave that place as soon as I lined something up. I just left a little earlier than I planned to leave."

"Is there anything I can do?"

Janet was quick to shake her head. She remembered the last time he *helped*. "No, thank you. I have some interviews lined up."

"If they don't work out, you promise to come and see me?"

Janet smiled. Working for him wasn't going to work. Even she saw that. "I have some interviews lined up," she said again.

Richard laughed. "You're a stubborn one," he said. And then the waiter brought her drink, and they placed their dinner orders.

When the waiter left their table, Richard decided to go there. He liked being with her. He liked looking at the expressions on her face. She intrigued him. "What about your love life?" he asked her. He needed to know. He didn't invite her to that restaurant for his health. He invited her to see if there was some *there* still there. He now knew it was there in spades.

If she was in a relationship, he was wasting his time.

But Janet was curious about his question. Why would he want to know something like that? "What about my love life?" she asked him.

"Are you seeing somebody right now?"

Janet hesitated. What was the correct response? To ask him why would that matter to him, and thereby get more of an explanation as to why he would care? Or to just tell the truth?

She settled on the truth. "No," she said to him.

Richard inwardly felt relief. But you couldn't tell it to look at him.

But two could play that game, Janet thought. "What about you?" she asked.

Richard looked at her. "What about me?"

Janet felt odd asking him such a heady question because she knew it would imply she had a chance with him. But if he could make that implication regarding her, she should have the right to make it regarding him. "Are you seeing someone?" she asked him.

Richard wanted to say no the way she had. Point blank period no. But he would be lying to her. And he wasn't going to do that. "I see lots of people, Janet," he said to her.

Janet's heart dropped. That was what she got for trying to grab for somebody so beyond her reach! What was she thinking? "I see," she said, and managed to smile.

But Richard saw the pain in her smile. And he couldn't handle that. "But right now," he said, deciding to rely on truth with nuance, "I'm not seeing anybody."

Janet looked at him.

"I'm tired of the hit and runs," he added, and then looked at her. "You know what I mean?"

She only had one experience with a hit and run, and he was the perpetrator. "Yes," she said.

And she did feel better, but his first answer had put her on notice. He had lots of females. That was what he was saying initially. Which made it clear to her that he wasn't interested in her that way. Which she should have known all along. But now she knew. Don't ever get comfortable with him, she told herself.

And as if they had conjured it up, they both suddenly heard a voice. One of his ladies?

"Hello, Dicky."

When he looked and saw Margo, who was indeed one of his lady friends with benefits, he wanted to tell her to scram. It was as if he was in delicate talks with a super power nation, where his happiness depended on the outcome of those talks, and some banana republic interrupted him. But there she was, with two of her girlfriends, standing at his booth.

Janet saw her too, and the one thing she saw about her, just like she saw with his secretary Doris, and probably every woman he currently had, was how beautiful she was. Which only served to remind Janet of how beautiful she was not.

"Hello, Margo," Richard said with no enthusiasm.

But Margo was smiling and looking at Janet. "Who's that, darling?" she asked Richard. "Your housekeeper?"

Why that little heifer, Janet said to herself, as Margo's girlfriends giggled at her little joke.

But Richard didn't skip a beat. "No," he said, "she's not my housekeeper. You're hers."

Margo smiled a puzzled smile. "I'm *hers*? What kind of sense does that make?"

"The same kind of sense that shit you just said made," Richard fired back.

Margo's smile left. Her girlfriends' smiles did too. "What's that supposed to mean?" she asked him.

"It means get the fuck out of my face," Richard said and stared her down. "That's what it means!"

And he wouldn't relinquish his stare until Margo and her girls got the message and left his booth. But not before Margo gave Janet the harshest look she could muster. But Janet smiled at her. *Yeah, he shamed your shameful butt*, she wanted to say. But she didn't go there. Richard had already said it all.

When Margo and her posse left, Richard looked at her. "Sorry about that," he said.

But Janet smiled. "She's mad at you. And you know what?"

"What?"

"You don't give a damn!"

Richard laughed out loud. "Got that right!" he said. He truly liked this girl!

But then he stared at her again. He loved her spirit, but he knew it came from a place of pain. "It doesn't bother you when others disrespect you like that?"

Janet gave him a sincere look. "I'm used to it, Richard," she said.

"But how? How do you get used to something that vile?"

"When everybody treats you that way," Janet said, "it's surprisingly easy to get used to that treatment. It's not news when I'm mistreated. Trust me on that. The news is when I'm treated well." She gave him a look of total acceptance of the truth of her life. "I'm used to it. Don't cry for me, Argentina. No big deal at all."

Richard tried to smile at her little reference to that *Evita* tune, but he couldn't pull it off. What she had said, that mistreatment was the course of her life, touched him to his core. Instead of smiling, or playing it off the way she did, he, instead, studied her. And he made up his mind. Just like that. He inwardly decided that he would never allow anybody to ever mistreat her again. God as his witness.

And after her drink and then their meals arrived, and as they ate and small-talked their way through dinner, he realized in stark realness that not pursuing her all those years ago was the mistake of his life. He could have had Janet with him all those lonely nights. But he had gorgeous bedwarmers instead. Nobodies he didn't care about, and who didn't give a damn about him. As he ate and watched her, it was a startling realization. He could have tried to change for her. He didn't even like his lifestyle! Why didn't he try to change? He was certain he would have broke her heart. But he didn't have to break it! Why didn't he realize that at the time?

Because he didn't. He just didn't. And it was a mistake.

He wasn't going to make that mistake again.

"You owe me," he said to her when they finished their meals.

But Janet had a sudden stricken look on her face. What was he talking about? Her drink? He wanted her to pay for her drink? She would in a heartbeat.

But she realized she was being irrational. That man wasn't interested in her chump change! "I owe you for what?" she asked him.

"The last time we spent the night together," Richard said, "was at your place."

Janet stared at him. "Okay."

"Tonight," he said, staring at her, "we're spending the night at my place." And he was looking at her to make certain she registered what he was telling her. "Okay?" he asked her.

Janet knew exactly what he was saying. And she understood what he meant. But she had never done anything like that before in her life. Except once. And for Richard to be her first and second time?

It was exhilarating. But terrifying too.

And she wasn't the kind of person who was down for whatever. She needed more information before going down that rabbit hole. "Why?" she asked him.

Richard continued to stare at her. Did

she not understand what he was referencing? "Why what?" he asked her.

"Why me, Richard? Why not that beautiful woman who felt confident enough to call me your housekeeper to my face? The one you called Margo? Why me and not her tonight? You love beautiful women. Everybody knows that. Why would you want to bother with me?"

A different expression appeared on Richard's face. An expression Janet saw as either compelling, or repellant. He seemed bothered by her question.

And then he exhaled. And answered her. "When I see you, Janet, all I see is beauty."

"Come on, Richard," she said with a *don't bullshit me* look on her face.

"Listen to me," he responded. "I'm not going to patronizing you, okay? I love your face, is what I'm saying. It makes me smile. I love your spirit. It makes me want to be a better man." Then he frowned. "The honest answer is that I don't know why you, Janet. I just don't know. But what I do know? I don't want it to be anybody else but you."

But Janet still looked perplexed to Richard. "And you decided this when?" she asked him. "Because two days ago, at that meeting, you acted like you didn't remember me at all."

"Oh, I remembered you," Richard admitted. "I definitely remembered you."

"But?"

Richard hesitated. "But I didn't want to put it all on the line like that."

Janet still felt as if he was talking around the point, instead of getting to the point. "Why not?" she asked him.

Richard hesitated again. Then he decided to just put it out there. "Because I didn't feel that I was good enough for you, Janet," he said.

Janet stared at him. Not in disbelief. But in shock. Utter and complete shock.

But all Richard saw was her lack of response. Was she so against the idea of being with a man like him that it repulsed her? He smiled and attempted to play off his embarrassment. "I guess you agree with my assessment that I'm not good enough for you, hun?" he asked.

But then tears appeared in Janet's big hazel eyes. And it stunned him. "Janet, what is it?" he asked. "What's wrong?"

"All my life," she began, but then she stopped to wrestle back control of her emotions.

Richard just sat there, his heart aching for her. What did he say that would render her teary-eyed?

"All my life," Janet began again, "I've been relegated to the back of the room. People ignored me. Or picked on me. Or tried to bully me. They used to call me horse face. Shit face."

Richard was shocked. "They called you those names?"

"When I moved in with the Henleys, my so-called foster family, yes. They called me those names every day of my existence with them. Or they just called me Jane, a name I hate to this day, or PJ."

"PJ?" Richard asked. "Why PJ?"

"It was for Plain Jane."

Richard stared at her. "Plain? There's nothing plain about you."

"It was their way of saying that they knew what beauty was, and it wasn't me. Which was fine. I didn't care what they thought of me. But if I were to be truthful, it does take a toll on what you think of yourself. Their putdowns took a toll on me."

Richard's heart began hammering. How could anybody think of her as anything short of magnificent, he wondered.

And Janet continued. "When everybody who's supposed to care about me are telling me that there's something wrong with my face, how was I supposed to look at myself? My face is what shows up in the world. If they're saying it's a bad face, or an ugly face, what am I supposed to do with that? Hide it? How can you hide the very essence of who you show up in the world as? But I guess I did retreat. Trusted no one. Verified everything. Which didn't help me, either, in the romance department."

Richard took Janet's hand and placed it in his own. "I had no idea," he said to her. "I thought men would see what I see whenever I look at you, and beat your door down to be with you. Better men than me, is what I envisioned for you. But that didn't happen?"

Janet shook her head. "No. Nothing of the sort happened. That's why when you said that you, that a man like you weren't good enough for me? For a girl like me?" Janet shook her head. And then she smiled that high-wattage smile Richard was beginning to adore. "It kind of made my day, to be honest with you," she continued. Then she smiled again. "Who am I kidding? When you said those words to me, it kind of made my life!"

Richard laughed out loud. He laughed so loud that Margo and her crew, who sat further over, looked at him with nothing short of disgust on their faces.

"What I'm trying to say," Janet said, "is that it felt good to finally be thought of, in a positive light, by somebody."

"Oh, I'm sure many men think of you in nothing but a positive light," Richard said, still unable to believe that men could be that shallow. Not realizing how shallow he had been himself. "The reason they may have stayed away is the reason I didn't pursue you. They didn't think they were good enough for you either."

Janet laughed. This sweet man! "I doubt if that's the reason, Richard," she said to him. "But I'll take it."

He continued to smile back at her, but then his look turned serious. And then he placed her hand in his hand again, holding it and rubbing it at the same time. "And what I said earlier?" he asked her. "About spending the night with me? You haven't given me an answer."

"Me?" she asked. "Spend the night with you?"

Richard's heart was in his throat. Was she about to turn him down? Did she still not believe him when he spoke of her specialness? He wasn't lying! Did she believe he was?

Then she smiled, alleviating all his fears. "I'll be happy to, Richard," she said.

And he smiled too, but he wasn't going to delay any longer. He called for the waiter and paid for their ticket, and then looked at her.

"Ready?" he asked, standing up.

"I'm ready," Janet said, gathering up her purse as he hurried over to assist her to her feet.

And as they headed out, and as they approached Margo's table, Richard placed his arm around Janet's waist. Around his so-called housekeeper's waist. Because nobody was disrespecting Janet ever again.

Margo saw that move of possessiveness Richard showed toward Janet, a woman she considered to be an unworthy vessel of any man's affection, and couldn't hide her disgust. Richard saw her disgust.

But Janet was right. He didn't give a damn.

CHAPTER TWENTY

Her Honda Civic followed his Porsche to a big brick house on the other side of Tulsa. As they drove down the long, winding driveway, Janet was shocked by the many layers to the house. That roof went on for days, it seemed to her, as there appeared to be so many different sections to that house that she couldn't keep count. Janet knew that Richard was a very rich man. But she never could wrap her brain around just how rich until she saw that house, a house located in a neighborhood that was filled with similarly-situated big, beautiful homes. She didn't realize people lived that lavishly in Oklahoma. She'd never seen that side of the world before in her life.

And she was about to spend the night with the king of that side of the world? Was she insane???

But she refused to overthink it. Even after spending that one, precious night with Richard six years ago, and what followed that next morning, he remained her shining example of a good man. A man who found her mother's photograph. A man who gave her a luxury automobile, and attempted to give her a major promotion. A man who held her all night when those nightmares she'd had all of her life returned. Why they returned that night, she'd never know. But they had. And he was there for her.

And as they parked in the horseshoe driveway and she got out of her Civic, she felt so out of her depth that it stunned her. And she still couldn't believe she'd agreed to go to his home and spend the night with him. But if not now, when? If not Richard, who? If she was going to lose her heart to any man, she wanted it to be to Richard, who showed her that he could be a very caring man.

He'd also shown her how he could leave her and never give her a second thought. But it wasn't as if he made any such commitment to her back then. He didn't. And he hadn't this time either. She had to remind herself that a man who wanted to go to bed with her wasn't saying, in any way, shape or form, that he wanted to be with her afterwards. She had to resign herself to that reality too. That Richard, despite his kind words, could very well make love to her, and then leave her once again.

But this time, she feared, he just might take a big chunk of her heart with him.

Richard got out of his sportscar and flapped his suit coat over his shoulder. He was amused to see how Janet just stood there staring at his big home. "What do you think?" he asked her.

Janet was nodding her head. "It's . . . It's not a small home, is it?" she asked.

And Richard laughed. "No, my darling," he said. "It's not a small home." Then he placed his hand around her waist again. "Come on inside!" he said, and escorted her in.

They entered into a home that Janet could only describe as amazing. "It look as though it's straight out of a magazine," she said as she looked at the checkered flooring in marbled tiles. At the double staircase that wind around to meet up with each other downstairs, and move apart from each other upstairs. At the beautiful furnishings and statues and Roman-looking columns. She looked at Richard. "Did you decorated all of this yourself?" she asked him.

"Interior design? Oh, yes! Decorating is my passion."

Janet was surprised. "Really?"

"Darling, I'm kidding," Richard said, and Janet laughed.

She playfully hit him. "Not funny," she said.

"But you're laughing," he said, which made her laugh more. He was such a likeable person, she thought. How could everybody she'd ever known refer to him as a vampire? He was nothing of the sort!

Not that she knew him like that. She absolutely did not. But if her impression of him was anything, she'd stand by her belief. He was nothing like that.

But all jokes were cast aside as they made it upstairs to his bedroom. His four-poster bed was so huge that it could not have fit into any room in her house, but she didn't even bring it up. She was too in her head about what was about to transpire.

And when he handed her one of his big, white dress shirts and told her to make herself at home while he went downstairs to make a few business calls, she did just that. He had clean linen up the gazoo in his massive linen closet and she took advantage of the opportunity by grabbing one and taking a quick shower before getting in his bed.

And when she did get in his bed, wearing his shirt, she inhaled that wonderful scent. His shirt smelled like him. His bed smelled like him. Like that fresh cologne scent, but also with that hint of cigar. It should not have been a wonderful smell, that combination. But because it was Richard's smell, it was.

And his bed was so comfortable that she felt as if the pillow had swallowed her head first, and rendered her drowsy. She wasn't drowsy before she laid down. Now she could barely keep her eyes open. It became so bad that, within minutes of laying down, she had fallen asleep.

By the time Richard made it back upstairs, she had been asleep for nearly half an hour.

But instead of being upset when he saw that the object of his desire was asleep, he actually smiled at her. And stood there staring at her. She looked so peaceful in his shirt, and in his bed, that she looked as if she belonged there. She looked as if she should have been there years ago. But that was his shame.

He showered, too, and got in bed beside her.

When he got in bed, it was enough of a disturbance that Janet opened her eyes. When she saw Richard, she smiled. "Hey."

"Hey," Richard said, smiling as he placed his head on the pillow beside her. They were both lying on their sides, face to face. "You were fast asleep," he said.

"Me? No way."

"Yes way," Richard said.

Janet smiled. "I couldn't help it. You

have a very comfortable bed."

"It's even more comfortable," he said, pulling her into his arms, "now that you're in it."

Janet snuggled closer against him as he held her. And it was only then did she realize he wore no clothes. Not a stitch!

She also realized how good it felt to be against his very firm, very muscular body. And his member was expanding with every beat of her heart.

Richard knew it too. Just being near her was making him rock-hard. He looked into her eyes. And he saw that she was feeling the heat too. And that was all he needed to know.

He pulled her all the way on top of him, wrapped his arms around her, and began kissing her. They kissed with an ease that was so special to Janet. She expected him to go for what he knew. Go rough. But Richard didn't do that. He was taking his time.

He was also taking his dick and massaging her vagina. He was getting her wet and ready, and reacquainting her with the feel of his thickness again.

But she wasn't that same twenty-two-year-old girl anymore. "Condom please," she said to him before things got out of hand.

Richard was surprised. He looked at her.

"And don't' remove it this time," she also

said.

Richard was a little hurt by her lack of trust in him. "I told you I've never removed a condom with anybody but you."

But that made no sense to Janet anymore. If he'd been so caught up in the throes of passion that he would remove a condom while being with her, a woman he had no intentions of being with long term, it would stand to reason that he would have removed condoms with other women he'd been with. "I know that's what you're telling me," she said to him.

"You don't' believe me?"

"I believe you need to put on a condom," Janet said with all sincerity, "and keep it on." She wasn't going to accidentally become anybody's baby mama. Nor anybody's AIDS patient.

Richard stared at her. Boy had she changed since the first time he was with her! But he understood her lack of confidence in him. He was the man who hit and ran on her. He reached into his nightstand drawer, pulled out a condom, and put it on.

At first, he just held her as if he were trying to decide if she was worth the effort. But he looked into her eyes. And those eyes, and her soft, naked body, harkened to him. And he began rubbing her small, tight ass, and his penis began expanding to a degree that it felt as if it was getting away from him. And he was all-in again.

He began kissing her sweetly, at first, and then passionately again. He moved her up slightly, unbuttoned the shirt she wore so that he could have access to her big breasts, and began sucking them as his dick began rubbing against her vagina again.

Janet felt nothing short of elation as Richard rubbed and sucked her. She loved the feeling.

Until he eased his penis inside of her.

She'd forgotten how thick it was.

It was so thick that it hurt her to her core.

It was so thick, and she was so tight, that Richard wasn't sure if he could contain himself.

And he couldn't.

Just thinking that it was Janet. Just thinking it was the woman he'd put on a pedestal for all those years broke his well-controlled will power and he rolled with her until she was on her back, and he was on top of her. And then he kissed her hard as he plunge his dick into her with such force of purpose that it caused Janet to lift her midsection up in an effort to force it back out.

But by then Richard had broken through

and was moving in further and further. Deeper and deeper. And then he started fucking her with a bed-bouncing fuck. He was moving it in and almost out, and all over again, as the pain continued to sear her. He was breathing so hard, and pumping so fast, that even she knew it was impossible for him to slow it back down. But he fucked her for so long, and with such passion, that the pain became secondary to her pleasure. Until the pain subsided altogether. And she was enjoying having him inside of her, and pleased with his thickness.

They stayed that way for nearly half an hour together. Making long, passionate, pulse-pounding love together. Until Janet couldn't hold out another second. And her orgasm took over. She felt the sensations up her spine and all over her body. Even her face felt the sensations. And it was even more intense than their first time.

And then Richard couldn't hold on, either, and he came just as fiercely. He felt those heightened sensations too. And he lifted his upper body, with the palm of his hands holding his muscular body up, and poured out of himself with such ferocity that Janet could see the veins in his forehead. And she came again.

They kept doing each other for several more minutes. Those feelings kept rolling within them and they kept rolling with those feelings. Richard was still pumping into her until the very end. Until they both ran out of gas, collapsing onto the bed, from the sheer weight of what they'd done.

CHAPTER TWENTY-ONE

For several minutes afterwards, they laid side by side without saying a word to each other. Richard was still feeling the effects of being with Janet again. It was that same feeling he had the first time he made love to her. That intense feeling of being finally satisfied. After so many tries with so many women, to be perfectly satisfied and perfectly thrilled.

But this time was even more special. This time, for the first time in his life, Richard didn't feel dirty afterwards. He didn't feel as if he was playing with somebody's heart, for his own heart's desire, simply because he could.

Janet, too, was thinking about the last time they made love. Her first time ever. And with the same man! And it felt great then too. But it was the aftermath that dampened it for her. It was the going to that drugstore. It was the way he hugged her goodbye, knowing he had no intentions of ever seeing her again. It was the pain of not seeing him again. The pain of not being in his arms again. The pain that came after the party, when everybody was gone, and she was alone again.

If her first experience with Richard taught

her anything, it taught her never to equate sex with love. It was this time, in the aftermath, after the sex, that she had to guard her heart.

Richard could feel Janet's openness closing as she laid beside him. And when he looked over at her, and saw that distressful look on her face, he knew why. He knew he needed to reassure her. This time was not going to be like the last time, he had to make certain she understood. There would be no disappearing acts on his part this time.

He found the strength and pulled her on top of him.

Janet smiled when she got on top of him and they were laying stomach to stomach and face to face. It felt as if she was laying on a chunk of steel.

Richard liked that she was looking at him and smiling, for whatever reason. And he smiled too. And rubbed her soft hair. "You're great in bed," he said to her.

She laughed. "Sure I am!"

"You are! Just as you were the first time."

"Now I know you're lying."

"But I'm not lying," Richard said, unable to keep a straight face. "Why would you think I'm lying?"

"How in the world can somebody with zero experience be great in bed? That's not possible."

"It is possible."

"How?"

"Because it's not about experience," Richard said, and his smile began to fade. "It's difficult to describe, but it's about that feeling you feel being inside somebody, long before you climax, that's just as electrifying as the climax. I've only felt that way precious few times in my life." He looked at her. "And both times were with you."

Janet felt her heart melt again when he said those words. He knew what words to say to her. But could she trust him?

She didn't respond to his flowery words. She just stared at his gorgeous square-jawed face and traced her finger along that jawline. And she laid her head on his chest. She was not going to let her need and inexperience, and his silvery tongue, dictate next steps. Her head, and only her head, was going to do that. She laid her head on his chest, and closed her eyes.

Richard saw that look in her eyes when she was tracing his jawline. He saw that she didn't believe a word he was saying to her. When he left her six years ago, it had to have hurt her. And he knew, if they were going to try to make this work, and he definitely was going to try, he needed to apologize.

"I should have phoned you, Janet," he said to her.

Janet opened her eyes but remained as she were.

"I should have told you I was sorry to have taken advantage of you that way, and I should have asked for your forgiveness. I apologize for that."

Janet hesitated before responding. Mostly because she didn't know what to say. She had no ready answer for an apology like that.

Then she leaned up and stared into his understanding eyes. And she found the words. "It would be so easy for me to just blame you for everything and accept your apology," she said to him. "But you really have nothing to apologize for. I was a grown woman who made the decision to do a grown woman thing. You made no commitments to me. You made no promises to me. You just wanted what you wanted that morning, and you took it. But guess what? I wanted what I wanted, and I took it too. Just because you had more experience at taking what you wanted didn't make me a victim. I was no innocent bystander."

Richard stared at her. "But you were hurt?"

"I was, yes. Deeply. But that was on me.

I was longing for somebody I had no business longing for. You hit and ran. I think you even told me that was what you did with women. So if a woman, namely me, decides to hop in bed with a man who already professed that he likes to hit and run, then that's on that woman. That was on me. You hit it and you ran. You did what you said you would do. I should have believed you."

Then she smiled. "But don't worry. I got over your ass."

Richard laughed. He really liked this girl! But then his look turned serious again. "Why did you return it, Janet?" he asked her.

Janet knew what he meant. He knew exactly what he was talking about. "I was accused of sleeping my way to that car," she said. "And that promotion. I couldn't live in that. That's why I left the mill. That's why I returned that Mercedes."

"And?"

Janet hesitated. Then she told the truth. "And, yes, I think a part of me wanted to get your attention. Maybe if I returned the car you'd see I didn't want your money or anything like that, and you'd want to be with me. And I know it was foolish thinking. But it was what a twenty-two-year-old girl would think. So, yeah, a part of me was hoping you'd phone. But you never did anyway, so, that was that."

Richard's heart melted. And he pulled her tighter into his arms. "I wanted to phone you so many times. I wanted to hop on my plane and come and see about you. But I wasn't a good guy back then Janet. I was deplorable. You deserved so much better than me."

"Apparently not, because I didn't get better," Janet shot back with what sounded like a twinge of bitterness in her voice. "Better? I didn't even get average. I didn't get anything. And I most certainly didn't get you."

Richard could hear the emotion in her voice. "I wasn't ready to have a woman like you," he said. "I would have used and abused you."

"And now?" she asked, and looked up at him. "What are you doing with me now? Are you using and abusing me now?"

Richard shook his head. "No. I'll never do that to you."

Janet smiled. "Can I take that to the bank?"

"My word? It's better than money."

Janet laughed. "We'll see about that," she said.

But Richard's look turned serious again. "You know the one thing I really admired about you the first time I met you?"

Janet looked at him. "What would you have admired about me?" she asked.

"When I came to that boarding house where you were staying?"

"What about it?"

"I loved the way you didn't make excuses. This was your life, and if I didn't like it, tough. I knew where the door was."

Janet smiled. "I'm sure that wasn't how I viewed it."

"But what I'm saying is that you didn't allow me to steal your truth. You didn't allow me to tear down what you had built up. Were you poor? Yes. Did you want to do better for yourself? Of course you did! But it was what it was at that time, and you made no apologies for what it was. I truly admired that, Janet."

Janet smiled. "Thank you," she said. "It's not everyday somebody says they admire me. Not *any* day, really," she added, with a laugh.

But Richard pulled her tighter into his arms. "Just like you got used to that shit the world was shoving down your throat," he said, "you're going to start getting used to the opposite."

Janet didn't know what he meant by that, but it sounded good to her. But she was going to let her head rule this time, and not her heart. "Tell me about you," she said. "And your family.

The famous Shetfields."

"You mean the infamous Shetfields, don't you?"

She laughed. "That too, yes," she said.

Richard exhaled. "There's my mother and my father, newly divorced and getting on everybody's nerves. And then there's my two brothers and me. My brothers and I are very close, and I'm close enough with my mother."

"And your father?"

"We don't see eye to eye."

"Why not?"

"Because I left the family business and went my own way. Because I'm wildly successful with businesses around the world when he only managed to conquer Oklahoma and Texas. Because he's an asshole whose ass I never kissed."

"But your brothers kiss it?"

Richard laughed. "Hell no. But he never expected them to."

"Only you?"

"Only me."

Janet stared at Richard. "There's something missing that you aren't telling me."

"You mean the part where he's convinced himself that I'm not his son? That bullshit? It's not worth bringing up."

But Janet could see the pain in Richard's

eyes when he brought it up. It might very well be bullshit, as he put it, but he had been harmed by it.

But Richard, being Richard, wasn't going to let that get him down. He placed his hand on the side of her face. "Don't you cry for me, Argentina, either," he said, and Janet laughed. Then he exhaled. "I'm good, Janet. I need no-one's sympathy."

Janet liked his spirit too. "Here here," she said.

But then, suddenly, something shifted between them. For several seconds they stared into each other's eyes as if they were seeing each other in a completely new light. Janet saw that Richard could make a great husband for her. Richard saw that Janet could make a magnificent wife for him. And a great mother for their future children. And it was a jarring realization for both of them. It was so jarring, and so alarming, that they both looked away.

And Janet began moving off of him. It was getting even beyond her definition of wishful thinking. "Time for me to go," she said.

Richard looked at her. "Go where? You're spending the night."

"Not tonight," she said as she closed his still-unbuttoned shirt around her naked body and got out of bed. She walked over to the chair where she had placed her clothes.

But Richard was perplexed. Was it something he'd said? No woman had ever turned down his invitation to stay the night. Or did that moment, where he saw her in a different light, frighten her?

He threw the covers off of himself, swung his legs out and sat on the edge of the bed. He watched as she removed his shirt off her body. A body so luring that he wanted to do her again. But she was too busy getting away from him. "What's wrong, Janet?" he asked her.

"Nothing's wrong," Janet said, putting on her clothes. "I just don't think it's a good idea for me to stay the night tonight."

"Why not?"

"Because I need to get home."

Richard felt as if she was taking him around in a circle. He felt as if he was begging her, something he'd never done before in his life. It was a feeling he'd never had before, and he didn't like having now. "What's at home that you suddenly have to get home to?" he asked her.

She sat in the chair and began putting on her shoes. "It's nothing that serious," she said. "I just don't wanna worry Mo," she added.

Richard frowned. Had he missed something? "Who the hell is Mo?" he asked her.

"The man I live with," she said.

When she said those words, Richard was floored. "The man you *live* with? What man you live with?"

"His name is Maurice Riley. But everybody calls him Mo. And if I stay out all night, even if I call him and tell him I'm going to stay out all night, he'll still be worried sick."

But Richard's face was a mask of anger and shock. "You live with a man?" he asked her.

It was only then did Janet bother to glance over at Richard's face. And when she saw that look on his face, a look of pure jealousy and hurt, she smiled. "He's not that kind of man, Richard, come on now!"

"How was I supposed to know that?"

"How? I just slept with you! You think I'll have a man at home and then hop in the bed with you?"

Richard had forgotten just that quickly that she was nothing like the women he was used to being with. Because yes, every one of the women he fooled around with would sleep with him in a heartbeat, and then go home to their men. But still! "Who is he, then, if he's not your man?"

Janet stopped putting on her shoes and thought about it. And then she told him who Mo was. "When I was four years old," she said, "Mo and his wife were my foster parents. But when his wife died two years later, they removed me out of his home and placed me with relatives. He wasn't even fifty years old at that time, but they claimed he was too old to take care of a little girl. But it had been the only good experience I had in foster care. And when I was able, I searched high and low for Mo and found him, dying from neglect in a nursing home. I took him into my house, took care of him, and now . . ."

Richard was staring at her. "And now what?"

"He takes care of me," Janet said bluntly. "He's seventy years old. I don't want to upset him."

It sounded just like Janet to do something as extraordinary as taking in some old guy just because he treated her well when she was four years old. Either that, he thought, or it sounded too good to be true.

He grabbed his cell phone off of his nightstand. "Give me your phone number," he said, "and take down mine."

Janet did as he requested and then he tossed his phone back onto his nightstand and stood up, careful to hold onto his nearly overfilled condom. "Let me use the toilet," he said as he began heading for the bathroom, "then I'll be ready."

But Janet was confused. She looked at him. "Ready for what?" she asked him.

"I'm following you home," he said.

"Richard, you don't have to do that."

"I know I don't have to do it. When did you hear me say I had to do it? I'm going to do it." And he went into the bathroom.

But as Janet listened to him pee, she couldn't help but smile. Was he going to see for himself that she was telling the truth about Mo? Was he actually jealous? But how on earth could a man like Richard Shetfield be jealous of some man in her house when he didn't even know her like that? Unless he was just the jealous type. But she knew better that that too. No hit and run guy would ever be jealous-hearted. It went against their very nature of not caring either way. Until that right woman came along who could change his nature. At least that was how it happened in the movies!

But Janet wasn't going down that yellow brick road with him again. There was no way she was convinced he found her special above all those beauty queens he was accustomed to. Women like his secretary Doris Wilson and that Margo lady from the restaurant. How could she ever compare to them despite Richard's glowing words about how he saw nothing but beauty in her? She was not about to let that man hurt her heart ever again. No matter what.

She was determined to stay on guard.

CHAPTER TWENTY-TWO

Richard drove his Porsche behind Janet's Honda and was still reeling from how he felt when he thought she had some young stud living with her. It did something to him, as if he thought for a second that she was playing him and was exacting her revenge for how he treated her six years ago. It wouldn't be out of the realm of possibility for the kind of women he'd dated all his life. He'd dated some vindictive bitches in his day. But the idea that it would be Janet pulling that shit upset him. And, if he were to be honest, hurt him.

He'd never reacted that way before in his life. Richard Shetfield jealous? Get real! But that was what it felt like. Pure, unadulterated, green-eyed jealousy. What was it about this girl? She brought out all these feelings he'd never felt before in his life. Good and bad.

But one thing for certain, he thought, regaining his mojo. This Mo person had better be old and decrepit, or Janet's ear was going to get an earful, and her ass was going to get a handful. Dick Shetfield was not the one to play with. Everybody knew that.

But nobody would believe that he would

follow a woman all the way to her home in another town just to make sure she wasn't bullshitting him about some man. He never cared before. He was the man who slept with her and left for six years, without even giving her a phone call. Why did he care now? He didn't know, he thought, as both cars turned onto a quiet suburban street, and drove up onto the driveway of a quiet, tiny-looking, cottage-styled home. But he did care.

He got out of his sportscar and walked over to the Honda just as Janet was getting out. He placed his hand around her waist again as they walked toward her front door, as if he still had points to prove. As if he wanted to make sure that if that Mo person was looking out the window, he was going to see that she belonged to Richard.

Janet loved every time he placed his arm around her. It made her feel warm and protected, and wanted without shame. Which was new to her. Men usually distanced themselves from her presence whenever other men came around, or else their buddies might think she belonged to them. Richard seemed to want them to think it.

And when they got to the front door, instead of letting her unlock the door, he rang the bell.

She looked at him. "Why would you do that?" he asked her.

"Let Mo answer it," he said to her.

"Why?"

"Why not? Why would you care who answers it? Why would you care if eeny-meeny-miny-mo answers it? What difference does it make who answers it?"

"He's seventy, Richard," Janet said. "He might have been asleep in bed."

Richard hadn't thought about that. He allowed his anger to overrule his sense, and his automatic *me-first* go-to feeling to get in the way.

But then the door was opened, and Mo was standing there. He was a good-looking man. Richard would have preferred that he wasn't so great looking. But he was definitely seventy. She wasn't lying. She wasn't playing him for a chump.

"You lost your key, Baby Girl?" Mo asked her, although he was staring at Richard.

"No, I didn't lose it," Janet said. "I wanted you to meet Richard."

"Shetfield?" Mo asked.

"Yes, sir."

"Shit," said Mo. "What you bringing him here for?" Then he caught himself. "I mean, hello," he said to Richard.

"How are you? Mo is it?"

"Maurice, yes."

"Nice to meet you, Maurice."

"Likewise."

"I'll be in in just a second, Mo," Janet said.

Mo gave Richard another suspicious look, but then he went back inside and closed the door.

"Now are you satisfied?" she asked Richard.

"I was satisfied all along," he said to her. Then he smiled. "Yes," he said.

Janet smiled too. "Good."

Then Richard leaned in and kissed her on the lips. "Call me later."

"And what's wrong with your fingers?" Janet asked with a grin. "You call me later."

Another first for Richard. Him call a female? It had always been the other way around. And he preferred that it remained that way. Even with Janet. "The thing is," he said, "I'm a very busy man."

"Then don't call me," Janet said.

This girl! But that look she was giving him, that whimsical, smiling look as if she were enjoying every second of his torture, caused him to smile too. And give in the way he felt he'd been giving in since they hooked back up. "I'll call you later," he said. "How's that?"

Janet smiled too. "Better," she said.

"Now get inside," he added, slapping her on the rear, "so I can go home."

She laughed at his little pat, too, and went on inside, closing and locking the door behind her.

And Richard, completely satisfied, got in his vehicle and sped away.

A gray Chrysler 300 that had driven up after they had, stopped across the street and the driver watched as Richard slapped Janet on her rear, laughed with her, and then got into his Porsche and drove away. But instead of driving off, too, behind Richard, the Chrysler remained where it was. For well over two hours. As the driver stared at Janet's house. Until there were no shadows of the two people inside the house moving past curtains. Until every light inside the house appeared to have turned off and the inhabitants gone to bed.

And then the driver put on a pair of thick leather gloves, and got out of the Chrysler.

CHAPTER TWENTY-THREE

After Janet had showered and got into bed, she couldn't sleep for anything in this world. At first, it was because she was just that happy. Richard made her feel so alive when she was around him. Unlike she'd ever felt around anybody. And the fact that he might have been jealous of Mo? A man like Richard Shetfield jealous because he thought some young virile man just might be living with her? She was over the moon!

But after almost two hours later and he still hadn't phoned her, reality began to set in again. What were the odds of it being true? That Richard could finally want to settle down? It seemed possible to her, whenever she was around him, but now that he wasn't around, and hadn't phoned, forced her to take a far more realistic view. Because it happened to her before. The first time she met him, and slept with him, she was over the moon then too. And he seemed to be sharing her excitement. He even drove her to work. And hugged her goodbye. Then, the same day, he buys her that luxury car and have a man find what appears to be the only photograph in existence of her long-deceased mother. Not to mention that incredible promotion he was dangling in front of her. She thought all of that had to have meant that he was over the moon about her too.

But he wasn't.

He not only never phoned her again for all of those six years, but he didn't have one of his people phone her to tell her something. As if he had gotten a spin with a virgin, and the fun for him was over.

And tonight, he had slept with the woman whose virginity he had taken, and he, once again, hadn't bothered to phone. As he said he would. Was the fun over for him again? Had she read too much into him again? She had no clue about these games people played in the romance department. She'd never had a romance outside of Richard. And you couldn't call that a *romance* anyway.

And the tears came again. He certainly knew how to make her cry, she thought. He was good at that too!

But it was her own damn fault, and she knew it.

She turned onto her side, turned off her light, and cried in the dark. Not for losing Richard. She never had him to lose him! But for what she thought could have been with Richard if he'd only given it a chance. And she cried silently, so Mo wouldn't hear her and think even less of those Shetfields than he already did.

Oh, God, she cried into her pillow, *why is there no happiness in this world for me too? What have I done my whole life to deserve so little? I know Richard is above my reach. But he's the only one who's ever bothered to reach for me. And then for him to build up my hopes again, and then dump me again, was excruciating this time. Because I should have known better. But I still allowed myself to hope*!

She felt like a fool.

A zip-dang fool, as Mo would call it.

Until her cell phone began ringing.

She lifted her head from the pillow and looked over at her phone as it lit up on her nightstand. And then she lifted her phone and looked at her caller ID. Saw the name Richard on her screen, given that was the name she had put in her Contacts when she put his number in her phone. And she hesitated. She could always refuse to answer and be spared the *I don't think we should see each other again* dumping lecture from him. But that wasn't her. She couldn't sweep things under a rug and just forget about them. Either way, she had to face facts. She wiped her tears away and answered the phone.

"Hello?"

"Did I wake you?"

"No. No, you didn't. You made it home safely?"

"Yes."

"It took you long enough."

There was a hesitation. "I guess so."

But he gave no explanation for why a twenty-minute drive back to Tulsa ended up taking two hours. But, apparently, he didn't feel he owed her an explanation because he didn't give one.

"What were you doing?" he asked her.

"I'm in bed."

"Wish I was there."

Janet didn't know what to say to that. He didn't ask to be there when he followed her home. It never even came up, or she would have let him stay.

"What are you wearing?" he asked her.

"Excuse me?"

"What are you sleeping in?" Richard asked. "Something, or nothing?"

Janet felt some kind of way about that question. Was their relationship predicated on sex alone? Was that the beginning and end of his interest in her? "I wear pajamas to bed," she said to him.

"Not sexy, but okay," Richard said.

He wasn't trying to camouflage it either, Janet thought. "Anyway, I'd better get some sleep," she said.

"Yeah, me too," Richard said. "I meet with the lawyers tomorrow. Good night, Janet."

"Good night," Janet said, and they ended the call.

She sat her phone back on the nightstand and turned onto her back. He called her. He kept his word. But it wasn't the kind of conversation she was hoping for. It wasn't a reassuring call as if they still stood a chance. It was just all sex talk.

"Who was it?"

Janet leaned up when she heard Mo's voice. He was standing in her doorway.

"Didn't mean to startle you," Mo said. "Was that him?"

Janet laid back down. "It was him."

Mo stared at her. Then he walked over and sat on the side of her bed. "He called you. But you don't seem happy about it."

"No. I guess I don't."

"Why not?"

Janet hesitated. "He seemed more interested in my body," she said, "than in me. Or maybe I'm reading too much into it."

"You're reading too much into it," he said.

Janet looked at him. "Why are you

saying that?"

"Because every man interested in a woman is interested in sex first. We just are. But here's the trick: how does he treat you when you're around him? Does he try to act like he's not with you when people come around? Does he laugh at your jokes? Does he pay the tab? Does he follow your ass all the way home just to make sure you aren't shacking up with some man?"

Janet smiled. "Shacking up?"

"Living with a man," Mo made it clearer. "Does he worry about that? Because I will tell you, if any of that other stuff is true, then yeah, he's interested in what your body can do for him. But he's interested in you too."

"But six years ago, I thought he was interested too," she said. "But he wasn't."

Mo looked at her. "You knew him six years ago?"

Janet had forgotten that she never told Mo the story. Not because she didn't want to, but because she was ashamed. "Yes," she said. "But only for one night."

"Oh, okay," Mo said. "Got it. Six years ago you guys hooked up and for him, it was a one-night stand, which was what it was. But to your inexperienced butt, you thought it was going to be a lifetime commitment. Right?"

Janet smiled. It sounded so crazy when Mo said it. "Right," she said. "That's what I thought."

"Wrongheaded thinking, Janet. Stop making it out to be more than it is. Just let it be what it is. Because he likes you. I saw that right off. Any man that would follow you all the way home just to see who you're living with is a man interested, not just in your body, but in you too. Bank that. Mo knows what he's talking about."

Janet smiled, and then leaned up and hugged Mo. And the tears returned as Mo returned her hug. She didn't know if he spoke the truth. Maybe Richard was interested in more than what he could get from her in the bedroom, or maybe it was just the bed.

But either way, she was worried. Either way, she was taking a risk.

Then they stopped embracing, she wiped her tears away, and Mo stood up. "Get some sleep," he said.

"And?" she asked when she realized he was lingering.

"And be careful," he said to her. "You're playing in the big leagues now, Baby Girl. Bigger than any league in town. I don't want to see you get squashed like a bug."

Janet smiled. Leave it to Mo. "Neither do I," she said.

Mo smiled, looked as if he pitied her again, and then left her room.

She laid back down. The last thing she wanted was anybody's pity. And sleep became as elusive as Richard's heart.

CHAPTER TWENTY-FOUR

Richard, in Armani head to toe, arrived at his office in downtown Tulsa that next morning, to meet lawyers about those allegations at the mill, but he had only one thing on his mind: Janet. He wanted to phone her when he first got up that morning, but he didn't want to disturb her had she still been asleep. Then he wanted to phone her on the way to work, but he couldn't bring himself to do so. He didn't want to come across as some desperate old man trying to be with the vibrant young woman. Because he felt that was how he came across last night when he phoned her later, and it bothered him all night. What was his problem? Was it self-sabotage?

But just thinking about her now put a smile on his face. Especially when he thought about that moment last night when he saw her as his wife. As the woman he wanted to be the mother of his children. And that was the best feeling of all. He couldn't wipe that smile from his face.

Even Doris Wilson, his secretary, could see that he was in an uncharacteristically good mood when he entered his office suite. "You seem pleased with yourself," she said as she followed him into his huge office.

"It's a beautiful day," Richard said as he walked.

"It was a beautiful day yesterday, and the day before that," Doris said as they headed for his desk. "You couldn't care less those days."

"Well I care today," Richard said as he made his way around his desk. "How's that?"

"That's good," Doris said. "Now sign these." She plopped a stack of papers onto his desk.

"And what are these?" Richard asked, sitting his briefcase down.

"Vendor contracts. All up for renewal. And mill management contracts, of course."

Richard's smile left, and he sat down. "Don't mention that mill," he said as he began reading over each contract before he would sign. "What time are the lawyers scheduled to be here?"

"By eleven. I told you we should have went with them in the first place."

"Not to settle," Richard said. "I'm not settling this case. I want to make it clear to them that I don't even want settlement talks. I plan to take those assholes all the way to the Supreme Court if I have to. I gave up a mini-fortune on those other complaints by settling out of court.

I'm done with that."

"Yes, sir." And then she handed him a pen. And he dutifully signed the contracts, and handed them back to Doris.

"Thank you, sir," she said and was about to say more. But Richard couldn't wait another second. He had already pulled out his cell phone and was making a call. Doris waited.

Janet was in her Honda driving along the highway. Her job interview happened to be in Tulsa, too, and she was nearing its city limits when her cell phone rang.

She answered the call without looking at the Caller ID. "Hello?"

Richard leaned back and smiled when he heard her voice again. "Hey there."

Janet was surprised. "Hi."

"How are you this beautiful morning?"

Janet smiled. He sounded much better than he did last night, she thought. "I'm good," she said. "And you?"

"I'm fantastic," said Richard.

"Where are you? Still home?"

"I'm at the office. What about you?"

"I have a job interview."

"A job interview? Where?"

"It's in Tulsa. I'm on my way there now."

"What kind of job?"

"Consulting," Janet said as she realized she was driving above the speed limit and attempted to slow it down. She pressed on her brake, but her car continued to accelerate. Baffled, she pressed on her brake again, and the brake gave way and went all the way to the floor. Now she was panicking.

"I don't have any brakes, Richard," she said nervously, pressing on the brakes over and over.

Richard wasn't sure if he heard her right. "You what?" he asked her.

"Richard, I don't have any brakes!" she screamed.

Richard jumped up from his chair so fast that the chair fell backwards. "Where are you?"

"On Route 9," Janet said, still slamming on the brakes. "I don't have brakes. I don't have any brakes!"

"Call 911," Richard yelled to Doris as he began running for the exit. "She's on Route 9 in a black Honda Civic."

"What's wrong?" Doris asked anxiously.

"No brakes!" Richard said as he ran out of the office. Doris was running behind him, calling 911.

"Don't put your feet on the gas!" he said to Janet.

"It's not on the gas," Janet yelled back at

him. She was hysterical.

"Pump the brakes. Have you been pumping the brakes?"

She'd been slamming on them. She tried to pump them.

"Janet!" Richard yelled as he ran into the stairwell and began running down the stairs. "Pump the brakes!"

"I'm pumping them! I'm pumping them!"

"Still nothing?"

"Nothing. It won't stop, Richard. It won't stop!" Her car kept careening along the downward-sloped highway. She could hardly breathe she was so terrified.

"You know where your emergency brakes are?" Richard asked her.

She nodded her head. "Yes."

"Apply them now," Richard said, his heart hammering as he flew down stair after stair, skipping two-to-three as he ran. "Oh, God! Oh, God! Oh, God!"

Janet applied her emergency brake, but the car continued to drive full speed ahead. "That's not working, either, Richard! That's not working! I'm gonna put it in neutral."

"Do it," Richard said, although he knew that wouldn't do much either.

Janet put it in neutral. But it did little to stop the acceleration. And she saw an intersection ahead of her, and cars were going through that intersection. "I'm approaching an intersection," she declared. "Cars are in that intersection, Richard. I see cars driving through that intersection!"

"Start blowing your horn," Richard yelled. "Turn on your hazard lights and start blowing your horn!"

She did as he said, leaning her whole body onto her horn as she drove. But as she blew through the stop sign and was about to enter the intersection, a car that was entering it at the same time slammed on brakes, just barely avoiding a collision, and she was able to fly on through.

"I got through it," Janet said, unable to regulate her pounding heart. "Praise God I got through it. But it's not slowing down, Richard. Somebody did something to it. It won't slow down!"

Richard felt as if he was going to die where he stood, but he knew he couldn't give up. He continued to run downstairs.

"Is she still on Route 9?" Doris anxiously asked him.

"You're still on Route 9?" he asked her.

"I'm still here, yes."

He could hear Doris tell 911 that the Honda was still on Route 9. But his focus was on getting that car stopped. "Do you see those guardrails?" he asked her.

"They're pass the railroad tracks, but I see them."

"When you get near them you've got to force your car off the road and ram into those guardrails, you hear me?"

"Okay."

"But sideswipe them," he said, "or you could lose traction."

"Oh, no," Janet said, looking ahead.

"Oh no what?"

"Dear Lord."

"What is it, Janet?" He had flown through the lobby and was outside running for his car. "What is it?"

"A train's coming, Richard. There's a train on that track and I'm heading straight for it!"

Richard's heart almost exploded. "Turn it!" he yelled at her in a voice beyond panic. "Turn it around! Turn that motherfucker around!"

And just as Janet was about to fly across those tracks for what would be a certain collision with that fast-moving Amtrak train, she clutched her steering wheel and turned it as fast and as far as she could turn it. She knew she was risking it all, but she also knew she had no choice.

And when she slung that steering wheel into a turning motion at that high rate of speed, her car couldn't take it. She avoided the train, alright, as it sped on by, but her car tilted sideways on two wheels, and then flew up, and slammed down flipping and flipping. It couldn't stop flipping.

Richard heard the sound of the train, and then the sound of a car crashing violently. He thought he was going to die. Janet?" he was yelling as he jumped in his car. "Janet! Janet! *Janet*!"

And then, suddenly, he heard no sound whatsoever. And that terrified him most of all.

He sped so fast out of that parking lot that his Porsche nearly swerved out of control.

CHAPTER TWENTY-FIVE

The ambulance and police cars clogged the highway that caused a massive backup of impatient drivers. At the back of the line, Richard jumped out of his Porsche, leaving the door wide open, and ran as fast as he could to where Janet's Honda ended up. Expecting to see her car wrapped around a train, he instead saw her car upside down and police frantically applying the jaws of life to break open the door.

But he couldn't see Janet from where he stood. And he had to see Janet.

He knelt beneath the police tape and tried to hurry toward the wreckage, but he kept getting thwarted as policemen kept attempting to hold him back, insisting that no civilians were allowed. But he pushed one aside and tackled another one, determined to see for himself what had become of Janet.

Two other officers tried to pull him back,

too, until they realized who he was. "That's Richard Shetfield," one of them said, and just hearing that name caused the rest of the officers to back off.

And Richard stood alongside the men trying to pry open that car door.

But he was near the back of the car and couldn't see up front. He hurried around the other side, to see if he could see on the end, but that was when the cops pried the door open. And they quickly pulled Janet from the rubble.

Richard ran back around to the other side and stopped all movement when he saw her. To his amazement and joy beyond measure, she wasn't harmed. She was standing on her own two feet and appeared not to have a scratch on her body. He was so astounded, and so overwhelmed with relief that he dropped to his knees.

When Janet saw that Richard was on the scene, she broke free from her rescuers and ran to him. She knelt down, too, where he was, and fell into his arms.

"You're okay," he kept telling her as he held her and rubbed her hair. "You're okay. You're going to be okay!" It was as if he was convincing himself.

But even he could feel them both trembling with fear. It had been that close!

When they stopped embracing, the paramedics hurried over and were asking Janet all kinds of questions. Then one said, "let's get you to the hospital so they can run some tests," but Janet was already shaking her head.

"I'm fine," she said.

"They need to run tests to be certain," said Richard.

"But I don't want to go to any hospital."

"I don't care what you want," Richard said firmly, still holding her. "You need to go and let them check you out. And guess what? You're going. And I'm going with you."

It was a relief that he'd be by her side, but it still felt unnecessary to Janet. She didn't want to go to any hospital! But she also knew how close she came to becoming that squashed bug Mo always loved to talk about. She knew she was in no emotional state to make any decisions. How could she decide anything when she couldn't even stop herself from shaking? She let Richard decide. And he already had.

She went to the hospital.

CHAPTER TWENTY-SIX

Later that evening, after the hospital visit and all tests had been completed, they were back at Richard's house. She sat on his sofa sipping tea while he paced the floor making phone call after phone call. And his command was the same to everybody he spoke to: he wanted to know who tampered with those brakes, and he wanted to know now!

The police already determined that it was no mechanical failure and that the brakes and other car components had been tampered with. They said it was a miracle she survived it. Janet and Richard thanked God.

And Richard, Janet noticed, couldn't keep still. He was so upset that it kept her on edge too. Who would tamper with her brakes? Nothing that crazy had ever happened to her before, until after she slept with Richard.

Richard seemed to realize it, too, and felt guilty about it, because he was on that phone letting his people have it, as if they were somehow responsible for allowing it to happen when there was no way they could have saw this coming. But that was Richard, Janet was beginning to understand. He could be difficult.

He wasn't an easy man to work for any day of the week.

His intercom buzzed just as he was ending another one of those shouting match phone calls, and he hurried over to the side table next to Janet and pressed a button. Janet hadn't even realized a button was on that table.

"Yes?" Richard's voice dripped with impatience.

"Spencer Shetfield, and Miss Fiona, are here to see you, sir."

It was the guard on the gate. Normally he didn't have one guarding the gate. But after what happened with Janet, he was taking no chances.

And he looked at her. He was still shook-up himself. He knew she had to be. Was she up for company? "That's my kid brother, the one that lives here in Tulsa, too, and his fiancée. You feel like seeing people right now?"

Janet truly didn't. But it was Richard's home and Richard's family. "Are you up to it?" she asked him.

"Not really, no. But he means well. He thinks highly of you. I'll see to it that they don't stay long."

Janet nodded her head. "Okay," she said, and Richard allowed them passage in. But Janet was surprised by what Richard had said.

How would his brother know anything about her? And why would he think highly of her?

But before she could ask Richard either of those questions, she saw a nice-looking white guy who appeared to be in his early thirties, along with a white woman who was almost as small as Janet, walk in. And the guy hurried toward the sofa, with the girl lagging behind.

"I told you she was okay," Richard said as Spencer hurried over.

"I wanted to see for myself," Spencer said. "Your idea of okay may not be my idea of okay." Then he reached out his hand to Janet. "Hi," he said with the most charming smile, "I'm Spence Shetfield. I'm sure my brother has told you loads about me."

Janet had been told next to nothing about him. "Nice to meet you, Spence," she said. "I'm Janet Evans."

"Yes, I know," he said as if it was an obvious fact. And he kept staring at her with a grin on his face. So much so that his fiancée cleared her throat.

"Oh, right," Spencer said, moving aside so that his lady could get some attention too. "This is Fiona, my fiancée. Fiona, meet Janet."

Both women smiled as they shook hands. "Nice to finally meet you," Fiona said.

"You too," Janet said, although she had

never even heard that name before. But both Spence and Fiona were carrying on as if Richard had been talking about Janet for years. Which would be wonderful, Janet thought, if that were true.

"You must have been terrified," Fiona said as she sat next to Janet. "No brakes? Oh my goodness! That had to be horrifying for you."

"Yes, it was."

"When Spencie told me about it, I told him to take my Lexus to the dealership right now and have it checked from top to bottom. But when he told me you were driving a Honda Civic, I told him never mind."

Janet waited for her to explain why she would have said never mind, but she never did explain it.

Richard looked at his brother. Fiona always had a way of grating on his nerves. "I know, I know," Spencer said low enough for only his brother to hear. "She may not be the sharpest knife in the drawer, but she's loveable."

But as Fiona kept going on and on about what happened and how terrible it was, Janet began to feel that surge of panic again. And she suddenly stood up.

Spencer was shocked at how quickly his brother reacted to her mere standing up. Fiona was too.

"Are you okay?" Richard asked anxiously, hurrying to her.

"Oh, I'm fine, Richard, thank you. I just think I need to lay down for a few minutes."

"Yes, of course! I'll walk you upstairs."

"No, please don't. Stay down here with your company. I'm fine," she added, said her goodnights to Spencer and his fiancée, and then made her way upstairs.

Spencer watched Richard as Richard stared at Janet. When Janet was out of sight, Richard exhaled and rubbed his neck. Spencer could see the distress all over his face.

"She's nothing like I thought she would be," Fiona said with a grin on her face.

Both brothers looked at her. "How did you think she would be?" Spencer asked her.

"I don't know," Fiona said with another grin. "Beautiful?"

Spencer's forehead lifted at the very thought that she would diss Richard's lady like that, and do so in Richard's face. He looked at his brother quickly. He knew how menacing Richard's temper could be.

It was obvious by the look on Richard's face that he was pissed with Fiona, a woman he had little regard for in normal circumstances. But Spencer could also tell his brother had bigger things on his mind than to even entertain her little comment.

And Spencer decided to move on too. "Who would have tampered with her brakes?" he asked his brother. "That's some scary shit. Who would pull that off?"

Richard shook his head. "I have no idea. But I want those bastards found."

"You've got men on it?"

"I contacted Darwin. He's got every man available on it." Darwin was the Shetfield organization's security chief.

"What about Janet?" Spencer asked.

"What about her?"

"Are they checking out her enemies too?"

Richard looked at Spencer with a frown on his face. "Why would she have enemies? Why would you ask me something like that?"

"You mean you haven't asked her?"

Richard realized he hadn't. "No."

"Because you just assumed they were trying to harm you by harming her?"

"That's what I assumed, yes."

"But Richard, why would they? You just hooked back up with her. There hasn't been enough time."

When Spencer said it, Richard realized it too. He realized he'd been so traumatized by how closely it came to certain death for Janet that he hadn't been thinking straight at all!

Spencer saw it too. "We'll get out of your hair," he said. "I just wanted to make sure you guys were okay."

"Thanks, Spence."

"Come on, Fee."

"Already?" Fiona asked. "We just got here."

"And we're just leaving." He looked at Richard. "I'll call you later," he said, and then he and Fiona left.

Richard, still shocked that he hadn't even considered the possibility that the perps could be enemies of Janet's, walked over to his full-sized bar and poured himself a shot of whiskey. He drank it down fast, sat the glass back on the countertop, and then let out a loud burp. He made another phone call, to Darwin, and then he headed upstairs.

CHAPTER TWENTY-SEVEN

Janet was lying in his bed, under the covers, when he made it upstairs. He folded his arms, leaned against the doorjamb, and watched her as she lay. It was still uncanny to him how much she appeared to belong there. But it was still sad to him, too, because he knew she could have been there six years ago, had he only taken that chance.

He aimed to rectify that error if it was the last thing he ever did.

Janet, feeling just as relaxed as Richard thought she looked, moved from her side to her back. And that was when she saw him standing there. "I didn't hear you come up," she said. "They're gone already?"

"You sound like Fiona," Richard said as he pushed himself away from the doorjamb and made his way up to the bed. He sat on the edge of the bed and continued to stare at her. "How are you feeling?"

"I feel good. I started to take another long tub bath," she added with a smile. She had taken a bath when they first arrived at Richard's house from the hospital. "But I knew it was just my nerves acting up on me."

"That was quite the ordeal you went through, Janet. Don't minimize it."

"I know it was . . ." Just thinking about it gave her the willies. "It was the worst thing ever, Richard. When I saw that train coming and I still had no brakes, I almost froze I was so scared. It was you, yelling for me to turn it, that made me snap out of it and do what I had to do."

"If you think you were terrified," he said, shaking his head. "When I kept calling your name and got no answer? I nearly died, Janet. I've never been more afraid of anything in my entire life. I thought I had lost you when I literally just found you."

Janet knew exactly what he meant. That thought had crossed her mind too. She thought she'd never see him again. And it was an awful thought. She reached out her arms to him.

Richard pulled the covers back, got in bed beside her, and pulled her into his arms. They held each other that way for several more minutes. And then they laid there, side by side, facing each other.

"I don't know why I got in your bed like this. I need to take my behind home. Mo's going to start worrying soon."

"You still haven't told him?"

"No. And I don't intend to. No brakes? He'll worry himself sick if he found out."

"But you'll have to tell him something. You don't even have a car any longer."

Janet laughed. "I forgot about that!" Then she thought about why she had no car any longer, and the smile faded.

"I have some bad news," Richard said.

Janet looked at him. "What?"

"You're going to have to tell Mo exactly what happened."

"Just because I don't have a car? I'll let him know there was an accident, sure, but I won't have to let him know the extent of what happened."

"He'll figure that out himself," Richard said.

Janet didn't understand. "And why's that?"

"Because you're going to stay with me from here on out, until I know for certain who those bastards are that tried that shit."

"But . . . stay here?"

"Or I'll stay at your house," Richard said.

"But either way, you're staying with me until I find the assholes responsible. Where I go, you go. From here on out."

Janet felt a sense of alarm that she would, in essence, need a bodyguard, but she also felt elated that Richard would be that bodyguard. Finally she just might have a man willing to look out for her. It was a strange-new-world experience for Janet.

"That includes tomorrow," Richard said.

Janet looked at him. "What about tomorrow?"

"I meet with the lawyers. I was supposed to meet with them today."

"About the mill?"

Richard nodded. "Oh, yeah. That hasn't been resolved."

"So you're going to settle out of court?"

"Absolutely not! I did that too many times before. I'm fighting it this time."

Janet gave Richard a look that let him know she wasn't exactly in agreement with that decision. "What is it?" he asked her. "You don't agree?"

"I don't know enough to agree or disagree. But I wonder if you know enough."

Richard frowned. "Why wouldn't I know enough?"

"Have you spoken with the workers yet?"

"Those females filing that lawsuit? No. And I don't intend to."

"Not them," said Janet. "But the workers in general. Those not a party to the lawsuit. They just might give you an earful."

Richard hadn't even considered it. He exhaled. "I guess we can pay the mill a visit before I meet with the lawyers tomorrow."

"We?" Janet asked. "What you mean we, white man?"

Richard laughed. "Where I go, you go. Remember?"

Janet smiled. "I remember."

"Which reminds me," Richard said. "I've got my security chief running a background check on you."

Janet was surprised. "A background check? What for?"

"Not to check on you, *per se*," Richard said, "but to check on any enemies you might have."

Enemies?" Janet asked.

"People in your past who may want to do you harm. Like Rooney and Rice for instance."

"Why would Rooney and Rice want to harm me?"

"Had they gotten that contract with me, I would have been, by far, their biggest client. You said William Rice blamed you for failing to close the deal."

"That's true."

"It's a long shot, but I want it checked out anyway. Can you think of anybody else?"

Janet didn't have to think about it. She was already shaking her head. "No. It never even occurred to me that somebody would have bothered with my brakes because of a grudge against me. I just assumed---"

"They were after me?" Richard asked.

"Maybe not after you," Janet said. "But upset with you for being with me."

"Like one of those women I fool around with?" Richard asked.

Janet nodded her head. "Like Margo from the restaurant, yes. That's kind of what I figured."

"I thought about that. And my guys are checking that angle out too. But time isn't on our side. It hasn't been enough time for word to get around about you and me, unless they were already snooping in my life. And besides, those women don't give a damn about me. They liked the gifts and bragging rights, but that's about it. There's a line of men in this town who can give them both of those things." Then he smiled. "No worries, okay?"

She smiled too. "Being with you makes life feel so different," she said.

Richard looked at her.

"Even in the midst of that traumatic experience," she continued, "I felt unburdened afterwards because you were there as soon as I stepped out of that car. That means a lot to me, Richard."

Richard smiled. "Your being here with me," he said, "means more to me than you'll ever know." Then he paused with a look that appeared anguished. Janet immediately wondered if it was because of her confession about him being there for her. Was it too much too soon for him? It was obvious, given his lifestyle, that he was commitment-phobic. What was she thinking?

But that wasn't it at all for Richard. Because he had a confession of his own. "I regret," he started saying, but then stopped. And then he started again. It needed to be said plainly, he felt. "Six years ago," he said, "I regret not pursuing you, Janet."

Janet stared at him.

And he kept talking. "I regret not giving it my all to make you mine. I should have. My life would have been so different had I made that commitment to you. But I didn't. I was certain I'd hurt you. I was certain I'd leave you. That's what I thought it was, anyway, all these years. But now I realize that wasn't it at all. I wouldn't have hurt you. I wouldn't have left you."

Janet was shocked to hear that. "Then why didn't you give us a try?" she asked him.

"The simple truth is that I was afraid."

"Afraid of what?"

Richard began rubbing the side of her face with the back of his hand. "You have the smoothest skin I've ever felt," he said.

"Richard!" She wanted a straight answer. "You were afraid of what?"

Richard exhaled. "I was afraid that you'd hurt me. That you'd leave me. And I wouldn't be able to come back from that."

Janet was stunned. She stared at him. She didn't know what to say.

Then she found the words. "I'd never hurt you," she said to him. "How could you have thought I'd hurt you?"

"I've never met anybody like you, Janet. I didn't know what to think. Or to do. I just knew I wasn't taking any chances. Even in my businesses I'm risk-adverse. I don't take chances, I just don't. I should have taken a chance with you."

Janet wrapped her arms around Richard, and he pulled her to him, hugging her too. "I won't hurt you, Richard."

"And I won't hurt you, Janet. We're in this thing together. We'll sink or swim together."

But Janet would have none of that. She pulled back and looked him in the eyes. "We'll swim together," she said. "No sinking. We can prevent that forest fire. We can prevent that drowning. It's up to us, and how committed we are to making this work."

He smiled. "You're so right," he said. "We'll swim together."

Janet smiled, too, and they kept their arms around one another, staring into each other's eyes, until Richard kissed her on her lips.

And that was all it took. They fell into a long kiss as they embraced each other tightly. Janet could feel Richard swelling against her, and Richard could feel Janet's heart hammering against him. Which, he now knew, was how she expressed her state of heat.

Richard was so caught up in the throes of their passion that he removed his clothing, removed his dress shirt that she wore, got on top of her, and ravaged her breasts for several minutes. So much so that Janet almost came from that feeling alone. They were so caught up in passion that he entered her, raw, and neither one of them said a word.

Janet knew she should have stopped him. But she was too caught up in the throes of passion, too. And when he started moving inside of her, and she felt him in the raw, she could hardly contain herself. She held on and enjoyed every second. They both enjoyed it. So much so that they even forgot about the incident earlier. And the all-day hospital stay. And they were no longer stunned by the fact that they both had decided to give their relationship a shot, which meant commitment, which neither one of them had any experience with. And even that was okay. Because they loved being with each other just that much.

And then Richard's self-control broke, and his slow-motion lovemaking changed, and he began to pound.

So much so that the bed seemed to move. So much so that Janet was screaming in elation. So much so that Richard came first and poured into her until his tank was nearly empty, and they still kept going at it. They couldn't seem to stop themselves.

Until Janet's cell phone began ringing.

"Get it later," Richard said, pounding her still.

"I have to get it now," she said, reaching for her phone. "It may be Mo."

It was Mo. He hadn't heard from her all day and wanted to know if she was okay. She said that she was, and that she was with Richard, and that she would call him back later. And then she tossed the phone aside, as

Richard continued to pound her and suck her breasts in such a way that she couldn't begin to think about anything but how wonderful it felt. And she began to have another orgasm. And he came again, too, just after she did.

It was later, when it was all over and they were wrapped up in each other's arms that they both reached the same conclusion: that Mo needed to be told exactly what was going on, and how little they knew why it was happening. And he needed to be under Richard's protection too.

CHAPTER TWENTY-EIGHT

Janet was right. Those workers, males and females alike, gave Richard an earful. And it wasn't just Lance Colvin that was the problem, they said. Most of management, which was all male, the ladies pointed out, treated the good-looking women as if they were their play-toys. They made those women section leaders or gave them all of the overtime, the workers told Richard and Janet, but they had to pay a price to get those perks.

"Perks," Janet said, as she and Richard walked out of the mill and stood at his Porsche. He opened the passenger side door for Janet. "They called them perks."

"I had no idea all that shit was going on," Richard said. "Was it like that when you were there?"

"No. Not that bad. I mean, Lance was an asshole. He truly was. But he was overall fair. At least to us regular girls. I can't speak for how he treated the so-called good-looking girls. I wasn't privy to any of that."

But when they walked up to the passenger side of Richard's car, and Richard opened the door for Janet to get in, he lingered

266

before letting her in. "You know what one of the lawyers phoned and told me last night?"

"What?"

"That if we didn't settle, the plaintiffs were going to mention the fact that I harassed you, too, when you worked here."

Janet was shocked. "*Me*? You never harassed me! Where would they get that nonsense from?"

"One of the ladies worked here six years ago and she remembered when I purchased that Mercedes for you and offered you that promotion to assistant manager. She remembered how it was all the rave at the mill. Mainly because you were only twenty-two, had just gotten hired, had worked in a meat packing plant for four years as your only experience, and suddenly you were going to be second in command. They said I was as bad as Lance."

"That's a lie," Janet said. "What you did for me wasn't harassment in any way."

"And if I go to court?"

"I'll be happy to testify to that fact. Although," she added.

As Richard waited for her to say more, he noticed a car parked down the street, on the same side as the truck stop café. Then he looked at Janet when she didn't continue. "Although what?" he asked her.

"If they're telling the truth about what's going on at this mill," Janet continued, "why would you want to fight that?"

Richard exhaled. "I have to, Janet, or every one of those ladies will want a piece of the pie too."

It was a dark gray Chrysler 300, he noticed. It wasn't on his property, but it was down the street from his property and looked odd parked there. And when it began moving slowly toward Mill property, Richard paid special attention. It was creeping along so slowly a couple cars flew around it. It was moving too slowly, Richard felt, as if it had other intentions beyond going from point A to point B. And then it suddenly began accelerating.

"Get in the car, Janet," he said , refusing to take his eyes off of that Chrysler. "Get in the car now!"

Panicking, she was getting in without asking him why. His voice made her understand the seriousness, and she didn't hesitate. But he pushed her in anyway as he pulled out his gun, ordering her to stay down. If those were the perps in that car, he was determined to get those bastards this time.

And as soon as he saw that the passenger on the backseat of that car revealed a rifle in his hand, he began firing first, running toward that car. He knew he hit the gunman on that hand because the rifle fell out of the open window. Now Richard was the one with the hardware advantage, and he aimed to use it.

"Stay down!" he yelled to Janet again as he began running across the dirt lawn of Mill property toward the street, running and firing at that Chrysler as it was speeding away. Richard was running as fast as he could, with an angle to cut that car off at the pass. And he didn't stop firing as he ran. He took out the back windshield of that windshield as he fired, with the glass shattering all over the trunk. And he also managed to hit one of the tires. But that was all.

The car still got away. By the time Richard made it into the street, that Chrysler, even with one bum tire and no back windshield, had turned a corner and was clean out of sight.

Richard was angry they got away, but he ran back to his Porsche to make certain Janet was okay. People in the mill were running outside, too, to see what all the fuss was about. But Richard didn't even look their way. He ran to his car.

"I'm okay," Janet said quickly, as soon as she sat up and saw that look of terror in his already overly-expressive big green eyes. "I'm okay. I wasn't hit. Did you see who it was?"

"No. I couldn't see shit through all that

tint on the windows. I took out the back windshield but by that time they were too far away. I did put a slug in the gunman."

Janet looked at him. She realized how little she truly knew about him! He put a slug into somebody? He said it as if it was no big deal at all.

Richard saw that look on her face. He knew it sounded strange to her, that he would be that proficient a shot, but she didn't know the half of it. He pulled her out of the car and pulled her into his arms. This part of his life, where he sometimes had to defend himself against some very unscrupulous characters, was a part he had hoped would never rear its ugly head around her.

But it already had.

Twice.

And he began to feel a surge of dread. What was he doing, he wondered, bringing her into his sordid life?

But she was in now. And he wasn't letting her back out. He just had to protect her.

No matter what the cost to himself, or anybody else.

CHAPTER TWENTY-NINE

They were at Janet's house. Richard was up front, yelling at his people on the phone again, and Janet and Mo were in Janet's bedroom. She was packing. Mo was already packed.

"You sure this a good idea, Baby Girl?" Mo asked her as he sat on the edge of her bed.

"He wants me out of town until he gets some answers," she said. They had already told Mo about the brakes. "He's worried I'm being targeted."

"But why would somebody be targeting you? Because you're with Richard Shetfield now and them bitches and hoes don't like it?"

Janet smiled. "I wouldn't call them those names, Mo."

"Then what you gon' call'em? Gold Diggers? Hoochie Mamas? Sluts?"

"*Ladies* was the term I was thinking of," said Janet.

Even Mo had to smile at that one. "Yeah, that too."

"And truthfully," Janet said, "I originally thought the same thing. That some lady that likes him might not like the fact that I'm with him.

But he's not so certain about that."

"He may be right," Mo said. "Those Shetfields have such a lousy reputation that it could be anybody."

Then Mo shook his head. He was worried for Janet. "All this violence around this one man. Makes you wonder."

"Makes you wonder what?" Janet asked him.

"What he done got himself into, Baby Girl."

Janet stopped folding a blouse and looked at him. "What do you mean?"

"I've been on God's green earth seventy years and nobody ain't never been shooting at me or jimmy-rigging my brakes. But you just got with this joker and already both of them things happened to you. Something don't smell right, Baby Girl."

"Just spit it out, Mo."

"What if he's a drug dealer?" Mo asked in a lowered voice. "What if that's the real Shetfield business?"

Janet was shocked he said that. Richard selling drugs? Was he insane? She rejected that notion out of hand. "There's no way Richard sells drugs," she said, and continued packing.

But Mo still wasn't so sure. "How would you know what he do and don't do?" he asked.

"You don't know him like that to be proclaiming what he will or will not do."

But Janet was still shaking her head. "He's no drug dealer."

"But what if he is? What then, Janet?"

Janet didn't stop packing, but she slowed down. She'd be devastated. Mo knew that. That was why he'd warned her.

"And now he wants to take you out of town to Texas of all places?"

"That was his big brother's idea," said Janet.

"His brother?" Even that sounded suspicious to Mo. "These people just met you, but you want me to believe even his brother cares about you too?"

"Not me. He cares about Richard. He wants Richard out of town until it all blows over."

"Blows over. Got you talking like a gangster."

Janet laughed.

But Mo was worried. "I don't know, Baby Girl," he said. "I need you to slow down and think this through. What if they are shady? What if you're getting yourself involved with some big-time unsavory people? I just want you to slow down before you get in too deep, okay?"

"Okay," Janet said, although her heart was already feeling as if it was in as deep as it could get in.

"Who all's going on this trip?" Mo asked.

"Richard and myself, his brother Spencer and Spencer's fiancée Fiona. And you, Mo."

"Oh, I already knew I was going when he said you were going. Where you go, I go."

"Quit lying," Janet said with a smile. "You never invite me to the casino with you and the Golden Girls."

"I said where you go, I go. I ain't never said nothing about where I go, you go."

Janet laughed. Then her smile eased up as the heaviness of what she was actually doing, and what had actually happened over the past two days, began to sink in.

Mo saw her changed look too. "What's going through that head of yours?" he asked her.

"I'm surprised you haven't asked why."

"Why what?"

"Why would a man like him go through all of this trouble for me? Why would he want me?" Janet said.

"Why would I ask you questions like that? Why do you want him is the question I'd ask! He's the one getting the prize, not you. Why would you want to be bothered with a man with a reputation for fooling around with all those different *ladies*, as you call'em? Why would you want to be with a man who has violence following him? Why him, is my question."

Janet exhaled. "Because I liked him from the moment I laid eyes on him six years ago. And when we came together again, it was like we had never parted. Like we were picking up where we left off."

"Except you did part ways six years ago," Mo said. "And you parted emptyhanded. He, on the other hand, parted with your virginity. Looks like he got the better of that deal."

"Depends on how you look at it," Janet said.

"What's that supposed to mean?"

"He parted after being given my virginity. He didn't take it. But that's true. I lost my virginity to him. But he gave me a brand-new Mercedes S-class."

Mo looked at her as if she had lost her mind. "A Mercedes?"

"A top of the line Mercedes."

Mo started looking around, as if it could be under her bed. "Where it's at?" he asked excitedly.

"That was six years ago, Mo! And besides, I gave it back."

Mo was stunned. "You gave it back? Are you brain dead? Who gives back a Mercedes-Benz?!"

"A woman who doesn't want her foster father referring to her as one of Richard Shetfield's hoes and bitches and whatever else you call them. A woman who preferred to get her own car, and keep her self-respect."

Mo nodded. "I hear you, baby. You was a fool, but I hear ya'."

Janet laughed. "Bump you!" she said playfully. "Just go get ready."

"I'm already ready." He stood up. "But I'll get out of your hair. Just one more thing though."

Janet looked at him. *Oh, Lord, what*, she wondered. "What?" she asked.

"When I was a young man," Mo said, "I was considered very good looking just like Shetfield is considered. And the thing about men that good looking? Most, not all, but most are not reliable."

Janet stared at Mo. "Were you reliable?"

"No," said Mo honestly. "Not in the least."

Janet's heart squeezed. And she continued staring at him.

"Don't get your hopes up," he said. "That's all I'm saying to you."

Janet nodded, and he left her alone.

Then she looked at the blouse in her hand, and she thought about how her life was so upside down right now that it caused her to

sit down herself. She had no job. She had
missed the interview she was going to when her
brakes went out. She didn't even have her
Honda Civic anymore. And now she was going
to go to Texas with Richard, and take poor Mo
with her? To meet the Shetfields? To meet the
vampires?

And the way Richard handled that gun. It
was like he was a police officer or somebody.
And the deference the police gave to him. It
could have been because he was rich and they
knew it. Or it could have been fear. Fear of a
drug dealer. Or an arms dealer. Or somebody
equally shady!

Mo told her she needed to slow her ass
down and not get her hopes up. Mo never led
her wrong. She slowed her ass back down.

CHAPTER THIRTY

Fiona was like a chatterbox the entire trip to Texas, but as soon as Richard's plane descended onto the tarmac in Arrowhead, Texas, a small town just outside of Corpus Christi, she started answering a text message on her phone and forgot all about Janet. Which was fine by Janet. Fiona was talking her ears off! And it was all about Fiona.

During that time, Janet would glance over at Richard, who sat a couple rows from them reviewing paperwork. He'd look up, shake his head and roll his eyes, making Janet fight hard not to laugh. And then she'd glance over at Spencer, Fiona's fiancé, who sat beside Richard, but he was completely ignoring her chatter.

At one point, when Fiona got up and went to use the restroom, Mo, who had been sitting across from Janet and Fiona, leaned toward

Janet. "Damn that woman can talk," he said, and Spencer heard it and laughed out loud. But Fiona came back and started talking nonstop again. So much so that Mo fell asleep.

He was still asleep as the plane taxied along the runway. Janet noticed a big, tall man, in faded blue jeans and a blazer, with a big hat on his head, waiting beside a Lincoln Navigator SUV, with a woman standing beside him with a cell phone and a clipboard in her hand. Were they there to meet their plane, or somebody else's, she wondered?

She nudged Fiona. After all that talking Janet had been subjected to, the least Fiona could do, Janet felt, was answer a question. "Who's that?" she asked.

Fiona looked up from her phone and glanced out of the window. "That's Montgomery," she said as she looked back down at her phone. "Their big brother. Isn't he dreamy? I can't stand him."

Janet looked at her. "Why not?"

"He's a pain in the gluteus maximus," Fiona said with a grin.

Janet smiled too. To know Fiona was to love her, even though she got on Richard's last nerve. Even though Richard told Janet how she made some snide comment about expecting her to be more beautiful, but that was nothing to

Janet. She'd heard far worse than that her whole life.

She looked back at the man Fiona called Montgomery. And the nice-looking lady standing beside him. She leaned toward Fiona again. "Is that his wife with him? Or girlfriend?" she asked.

"Is she white?" Fiona asked without looking away from her text messages.

Janet found that an odd thing to ask. She looked at Fiona. "Yes."

"Then that's not his woman," Fiona said.

Janet wanted to ask why not, since he was white, too, but she didn't bother. Fiona's answer could be sweet and to the point, or it could go on for days. Janet decided against taking that chance.

She, instead, decided to wake up Mo. And like every time when he was suddenly awakened, he sat straight up, with his eyes wide open, and started asking those same four questions he always asked. "Who? What? Where? Why?"

Fiona laughed. "You wake up weird," she said with a grin.

But Mo fired right back at her. "No you ain't calling nobody weird," he said, and Spencer laughed.

Janet quickly interrupted him before

Fiona could catch what he had said. "In any event, Mo," Janet said, "we've landed. Do you need to use the rest room before we get off?"

"I do, matter of fact," he said, looking crossly at Fiona. And he got up and headed down the aisle.

When Mo returned to his seat, Richard handed all of that paperwork he was signing over to one of his assistants who apparently flew with him everywhere he went, and then he went over to Janet and reached out his hand. "Come here for a minute," he said to her. She took his hand, stood up, and went with him to the back of the plane.

Fiona smiled and looked back at them as Richard took Janet into his bedroom aboard the plane and closed the door. She looked back at Mo, grinning. "He's taking her to his bedroom," she said.

Mo stared at her. "You sure know how to tell it, don't you?" he asked her.

But Fiona took it as a compliment. "Thank you," she said with a big smile. "Thank you very much."

Mo looked over at Spencer. Spencer, smiling too, hunched his shoulders. "She's gorgeous," he said to Mo. "What more you want?"

And Mo had to smile on that one.

But Janet wasn't smiling when Richard closed his bedroom door and they stood at that door. Because she knew it wasn't an intimate reason he took her back there. It was more serious than that. She could see the anguish in his eyes. "What's wrong?" she asked him.

At first Richard hesitated. At first, he was pulling her coat flaps together and rubbing the cashmere. Then he looked into her eyes. When he saw the concern there, he spoke. "I don't like coming back to this town," he said.

Janet didn't hesitate. "We can fly right back out of here," she said, "if you don't want to be here."

Richard looked at her. That was why he wanted her. She was a natural born ride or die. She would stand by him. "Don't you want to know why I don't like coming back here?"

"You don't like it," Janet said. "That's all I need to know."

Richard was so overwhelmed that he pulled her into his arms. And held her very tightly. "Thank you," he whispered in her ear. "Thank you."

He was more emotional than Janet thought she'd ever see from him, but it was still early days for them. And she held him just as tightly as he was holding her.

And then he pulled back. And that

anguish was gone. "It feels good not to have to carry burdens alone, you know?" Richard said to her.

Janet nodded her head. "I know," she said. "I feel the same way."

Then Richard exhaled. "I have two brothers, as you know. Spencer and Montgomery. All three of us have the same mother and father. But there are countless others in this town who are not my mother's children, but they're my father's."

"Did they become your father's while he was married to your mother?" Janet asked.

Richard nodded. "Oh, yes. Three, no, four of them graduated from the only high school in town, on the same day as I did," he said.

Janet was blown away. "Three or four of them?" she asked.

"Four, yes," said Richard. "And when Mom and Pop came to the graduation, those four graduates and even more kids went running up to him, calling him Dad just as bold, and he was smiling and hugging them and my mother could have fell through that floor. It was the first time she realized, and I realized, he had been cheating on her. But the rest of the town, and Monty too, already knew."

"Your brother knew?" Janet asked. "And he didn't tell your mother?"

"He never tells our father's secrets. And he never will. He accepts things as they are. I can't do that." Then he frowned. I hate coming back to this town."

"Then why did you come this time?"

"Because I needed to get you out of Oklahoma and around Monty, somebody I trust that can help me protect you. Because I need you to meet my parents and get it out of your system because I doubt if I'll be bringing you back this way again."

"Even to see your mother?"

"She stayed with Pop after my graduation. I asked her how could she stay with that monster after the shame he brought on all of us. Did she not have any pride about herself? But she said pride won't pay the bills. And back then, my old man held all the purse strings. She stayed for the money and the position. So, to answer your question, no, I won't be bringing you back even to see my mother."

Janet stared at Richard. He could be very vindictive, she saw that right off. But for good reason! "How many children, in total, do you think your father has in this town?"

Richard didn't skip a beat. "It was at least twenty when I was still living here. Probably way more than that now," he said.

Janet was floored. She'd heard of

mucked-up families before. Families like the Henleys. But not on this scale!

She pulled Richard into her arms again. "I'm with you, Richard," she said. "And we're a team." Then she pulled back. Was she being presumptuous? "Right?"

Richard smiled a heartwarming smile. "Right," he said. "And you're the boss of the team!"

Janet laughed. "Sure I am," she said.

Although Richard was smiling, too, he meant what he said. "Let's get this over with," he said as he kissed her on the lips.

But, as usual with the two of them, it wasn't enough to kiss and go. He was unzipping and pulling out, and unbuttoning her pants and pulling down, and then entering her.

He lifted her legs, putting them over his arms, and with her back against the door they made love on his plane for the first time ever. And the way it made Richard feel, and the headiness of it, caused him to cum early and cum first. He poured into Janet. But kept going, to make sure Janet came too.

And she did.

But by the time she did, he was spent.

He collapsed against her, causing her to smile, and she held him up. And then they cleaned up and returned to the others.

When they returned, Fiona stood up grinning and nudging Mo, with that *see, I told you* look on her pretty face. But Mo wasn't thinking about that woman as he stood up. He was thinking about the Shetfields he was about to meet, and if they were the drug kingpins he suspected they were.

Richard had butterflies, too, but for a very different reason. He just never liked going back home. It never ended well for him. But he was home now.

And he didn't delay any longer. With his arm protectively around Janet, they all deplaned.

CHAPTER THIRTY-ONE

Monty buttoned his suit coat when he saw his brothers and Fiona, and two additional people get off the plane and head his way.

His assistant, Donna, was looking too. "Who are they?" she asked.

"The old guy I do not know who he is. The woman," Monty said, "now that would be Janet, I suppose."

Donna looked at Monty. "Who's Janet?"

"Richard's lady."

Donna looked at Janet and then looked back at Richard. "Not his usual sort, is she?" she asked.

"Thank God!" Monty said, and then he stood erect as they were upon them.

"Hey, big brother," Spencer said. "Why are you working Donna on a beautiful day like today?"

"She doesn't have to work," Monty retorted, looking more at Janet than anybody else. "She won't get paid, but she doesn't have to work."

"Hello, Spence," said Donna. "Don't mind him."

Spencer smiled and gave Donna a peck

on the cheek. "How you been, little lady?"

"I've been great."

"Hello, Richard," Monty said, still staring at Janet. "I see you brought Janet Evans with you," he said.

Janet found it odd that both of Richard's brothers seemed to know of her far more than she knew of them.

"Yes, this is Janet. Janet, this is my old-ass brother Montgomery."

"Hi," Janet said with a smile and she and Monty shook hands. She didn't think any man could be better looking than Richard. She was wrong. Monty was, as Fiona had referred to him, *dreamy*. Even though she also said she couldn't stand him.

"And this is Janet's one-time foster parent, Maurice Riley," Richard said to Monty.

"Hello, Maurice," Monty said, shaking his hand. "Nice to meet you."

"Likewise," said Mo.

Fiona hit Spence in the back so hard that everybody heard the lick.

"Ouch!" Spence said. "What are you doing?" he asked Fiona. "He already knows you!"

"But he's ignoring me," Fiona whispered back to him.

Spencer looked at Monty. "And Fiona's

here. You remember Fiona, my fiancée, don't you?"

"Ready?" Monty asked, mainly to Richard and Janet.

"We're ready," Richard said.

"We been ready," said Mo, and they all laughed as they piled up in Monty's Navigator.

Donna sat up front with Monty, who was driving. Richard and Janet sat on the middle row, with Richard moving Janet so close to him that her shoulder was in his armpit and his arm was completely around her as if he was taking no chances with her security whatsoever. And Mo, Spencer and Fiona sat on the back row.

"Like stepchildren," Fiona was heard saying, but Monty ignored her the way he usually did, and took off. Like Richard usually had, he also had a cigar between his fingers, too, as he drove. But thankfully, Janet thought, his cigar wasn't lit inside the car.

But when they drove up to the big house, a house where the driveway was two miles long and snaked around until they were parking parallel to the main house, Janet and Mo thought they were in a movie. They'd never seen anything like it. Mo thought it was like a house straight out of Dallas or Dynasty. Janet thought it was straight out of Empire, with waterfalls out front and a statue of three horses in the circle at the top of the driveway. There were also a slew of expensive cars in the circle. It was all magnificent to see.

"Is this your parents' home?" Janet asked Richard.

"My parents? No," said Richard. "This is Monty's spread."

Janet looked at Richard. She was surprised. Monty was a little older than Richard: he looked to be a man in his early forties. And the idea that he owned so much land and beauty at his age was impressive. Did he have a wife, or children? Richard didn't mention it, and Fiona seemed to suggest he didn't have either.

When he stopped his SUV, everybody got out. It wasn't lost on anybody how possessive Richard was of Janet, especially when he noticed a certain car in the driveway. A Ferrari. "Dad's here?" he asked Monty.

"Apparently so," said Monty as he began making his way toward the entrance. "He apparently showed up while I went to meet your plane."

Janet could feel Richard's body tighten beside her, as they went inside.

Three people, Carter Shetfield and her ex-husband Fred Shetfield, along with his new, young, Russian bride, were seated at the huge dining table at the opposite end of the living room when they walked in, and Spencer and Fiona hurried toward them.

"Dad, Mom, hi!" Spencer said, thrilled to see them again.

Even Fiona was happy to see them. "Hey, Ma and Dad," she said. And they all hugged each other.

But Richard walked slowly with Janet and Mo into that dinning hall. Monty stayed near the entrance, giving Donna some final orders before she took her leave, but he was glancing at Richard too. To their father, Richard was the black sheep of the family even though he was as rich as Monty. But it wasn't about money with Fred Shetfield. It was all about respect. Monty and Spence respected their father. Richard did not.

"Hello, Dickie," his mother said as Richard left Janet's side and walked around and hugged his mother's neck.

"Hello, Mother," he said.

"You smell so good. You and Monty always smell so good."

Carter Shetfield had always majored in the minor details of life all Richard's life. He ignored it now. "I want you to meet Janet Evans," he said instead. And then he added: "My girlfriend."

Janet almost blushed when he referred to her in such an official way, and in front of his parents no less. And Carter smiled. But Fred Shetfield was staring at Janet.

"It's so good to meet you," Carter said as she shook Janet's hand. "You have such a nice figure," she added. "When I was young, I had a figure like that. Used to have to beat the boys off of me, yes, I did. I'll bet you have to do the same."

Fred Shetfield gave a one-syllable laugh that Janet and Richard both knew was meant to be snarky. And they both ignored him.

"No ma'am, I didn't have that experience," Janet said, "but it is so nice to meet you too."

"And this is her former foster parent, Maurice Riley," Richard said to his mother.

"Very nice to meet you, Maurice," Carter said as she and Mo shook hands.

"Nice to meet you, too, Carter. Strange name for a lady."

"I told my parents the same thing. But they said that's too bad. They agreed their only child would be named after my paternal grandfather no matter what gender that child turned out to be. So Carter it was when I was born."

"Not that it's your fault," said Mo. "Just

an odd name, that's all."

"You are so right," Carter said.

Then Mo looked across the table, at the big man and his young bride. If there was any drug dealing going on, Mo surmised, it was going to go through him. But he didn't look like the type at all. "You must be the senior Shetfield," Mo said.

"That's our father, Fred Shetfield," Spencer said because he knew Richard wasn't going to introduce him.

"Nice knowing you," Mo said to Fred.

"You don't know me, but okay," Fred responded.

Although Mo liked Carter right off, he didn't care for Fred at all. That guy, he felt, needed to come down a peg or two. He looked at Fred's bride. "That your daughter?" he asked Fred, and Carter laughed.

Fred frowned. "Does she look like my daughter? Of course that's not my daughter!"

"How was he to know? She's certainly young enough," Carter said.

"Stay out of my *got*damn business," Fred shot back at his ex-wife.

"Don't you talk to her that way!" Richard fired back.

And then silence ensued as the tension became thick in the room.

"Come have a seat beside me," Carter said to Janet, patting the chair beside her.

"Yes, ma'am," Janet said as Richard moved over and pulled out the chair for Janet. Mo took his own seat, in a chair against the wall.

"I wish I could say Richard has told me a lot about you," Carter said to Janet, "but he doesn't tell me anything about his life whatsoever."

"Nothing to tell," said Fred. "Following in his brother footsteps, as usual. That's all he has to tell."

Richard looked at his father. "What's that supposed to mean?"

"Just what I said. Montgomery likes black, so now you like it too."

Richard frowned. "Fuck you!" he yelled.

"Dickie!" said Carter.

"Come on, Richard now," said Spencer.

But Janet didn't say a word. Richard didn't respect his father, and for good reason.

Then the chef entered from out of the kitchen. "Dinner will be served in ten-and-a-half minutes," he said, and went back into the kitchen.

Nobody found it odd but Janet that the chef added half-minutes to the dinner time, but she assumed it was some rich people thing she knew nothing about. Mo didn't know it either.

He gave Janet a *what the fuck* look.

"I'll go wash up," Janet said, pulling back from the table.

"Fee, show her where," Spencer said to his fiancée and Fiona was happy to do something useful.

But as the two women were walking away, Richard was staring at his father, waiting for him to say something smart. Not for nothing was he concerned, but because his father could be a very cruel man. Because his father had that sneering look on his face as he stared at Janet. But only this time, his remark wasn't just some mild snarky comment. It was downright disrespectful.

"She's no Halle Berry, is she?" Fred said as he continued to stare at the retreating ladies. Then he looked at his son and smiled. "For you to want that," he said, "she must have some real good cunt between those legs!"

Before he could finish speaking, Richard's rage had already exploded and he jumped over that dinner table, grabbed his father by the throat, and they both fell over his chair and crashed to the floor.

"Dickie, no!" his mother cried, rising to her feet.

"Dick, don't do it!" cried Spencer, scrambling over the table, too, to break up the fight.

Janet and Fiona turned around when they heard the cries and Monty, still over by the front door talking with his assistant, saw it, too, and began running toward the scene.

Janet almost outran him and they both got in that dining hall at the same time.

By that time, Richard had his father down on his back. He had one hand around his father's throat and was punching him as hard as he could punch with his other hand. His rage was unleashed.

Spencer was on top of Richard, trying to pull him off their father, but Richard wasn't budging.

But Monty hurried over, grabbed Richard beneath his armpits, and lifted him up and away from Fred. But Richard broke away from Monty as soon as Monty had stood him up and leaned over to his father, even before his father, bleeding at the nose, could stand back up. "You will respect her!" he yelled, pointing angrily at him. "You will respect her! You will respect her!"

And the room went still. Nobody in that room had ever seen Richard defend anybody, especially some woman, in all his life. It shocked them all. Especially Monty. But Monty was shocked in a happy way. About damn time, he thought.

Janet wasn't shocked at all. She had come to expect him to be her protector. It was a natural fit to her. And she didn't even care what his father said that triggered him. All she knew was that Richard had already told her that she would never have to take anybody's disrespect ever again. That apparently included his own father.

She hurried to him. Although Richard was still seething, he placed his arm around Janet.

But as their father stood on his feet, seemingly too stunned to speak, Monty had the final word. It was his house, after all. "Time to go, Pop," he said to his father.

Fred was stunned. "What?"

"Get your girl and go," Monty said.

"You're kicking me out? Is that what you're doing?"

"Yes," said Monty. Even Janet could tell he didn't like doing so. "Just go," he said.

Richard could see that pained look on his father's face when Monty didn't stand up for him, since Monty was the only person in the world he truly loved, and he did as his oldest child told him to do. He got his young, Russian wife, and left.

And Mo made up his mind. Fred Shetfield was no drug kingpin. Not the way he took that takedown. But Richard? Now he was gangster, Mo thought. That was a real gangster.

He was going to keep his eyes on that young man.

CHAPTER THIRTY-TWO

Early that next morning, after a good night's sleep at Monty's house, Richard laid in bed staring at the ceiling. Janet laid beside him, on her side, staring at him.

"Your brother has a beautiful home," she said.

"Yes, he does. Makes mine look like a shack, doesn't it?"

Janet laughed. "No!" she said. "And he's not married?"

"Married? Monty? That'll be the day! No, he's not married."

"Fiona said he doesn't date white women."

"He doesn't date Hispanic women or Asian women or any other kind of women either. Except for black women. They're the only ones he bothers with. And he doesn't bother with them too often either."

"But why only black women?" Janet asked.

"That's what he likes. They're the only ones that turn him on. But as for me, I like'em all," Richard said with a smile.

Janet pushed him. "I'm sure you do!" But

then her look turned serious. "What did your father say about me?" she asked him.

"Ah, babe, you don't even want to know."

"Richard," Janet said. "Look at me."

Richard looked at her.

"Honesty between us, no matter how painful, is the only way this is going to work. You can't keep unpleasantness from me, and I won't keep it from you. Just be honest. That's all I'm asking. Trust me, I can take it."

Richard saw the sincerity in her eyes. But also the concern about what his father said about her. She didn't really want to know, he could tell, but she felt she needed to know. To keep her guard up. And he told her. "He said you're no Halle Berry."

Janet grinned. "True," she said.

"And what I'm attracted about you is apparently between your legs."

"Ouch," said Janet. "I can feel the sting of that! Although," she added.

Richard looked at her. "Although what?"

"It did cross my mind a time or two as well," Janet said.

Richard turned onto his side. "Why would you have thought that?"

"The first time we made love, remember? I expected to see you again. And I did. Six years later. Made me wonder if this was what that was too."

"And what did you think it was six years ago?" Richard asked.

"I thought it was exactly what it was," said Janet. "A hit and run."

Richard's heart dropped.

"That's what it was, right?"

Richard hated to admit it. "Yes," he said. "I didn't mean for it to be that, but yes. That's what it was. But how could you think that our relationship now is the same thing?"

"Because I was afraid, Richard. I was a hopeful fool six years ago. I thought we had made a connection back then, too, and the sky was the limit for us. I didn't pay attention to the fact that you looked depressed when you took me to that drug store to get that morning after pill. I didn't pay attention to the fact that you looked anguished driving me to work. And when Lance said you gave me that car later that same day, I just knew I had met the man of my dreams. And I kept looking all day and waiting to see you come to the mill to get me. But you never came. Nor did you call. That devastated me. It reminded me of that dream I had of my parents, when they left me too. I shouldn't have felt that way. You never promised me anything. Not even a phone call. But it still devastated me. And I knew that this time it'll be like beyond devastation if it turns out to be another hit and run job just like before."

Richard grabbed her and pulled her into his arms as if he was a very desperate man. "It'll never be that way again," he promised her. Then he pulled back and looked at her. "You said I didn't promise you anything the last time. And you're right. But this time, I promise you this: I'll be there for you. I'll never leave you again. I will give it my all to make this work. Just like I should have six years ago. But I just wasn't ready, Janet."

"But you're ready now?" Janet asked him, staring into his eyes as if she was searching them for any shred of doubt.

"I am ready now," Richard said, no doubt found. "I'm so tired of one-night stands and loveless relationships and women who only want what I can give to them. You want to give to me. And you have asked for nothing in return. But you're going to get plenty in return," Richard insisted. "Beginning with my heart. Beginning with my love. Beginning with being my woman, a woman every human being on the face of this earth had better respect. Or they'll going to answer to me. And that includes my family."

Tears were strolling down Janet's face. "And all of that, I'll give to you, too, Richard," she said, and he pulled her into his arms.

They remained that way for several minutes. The tears had subsided, but the commitment they made to each other was as real as air. And neither one of them felt uneasy. Or obligated. Or burdened.

They both felt remarkably free.

Until they heard a knock on the bedroom door. Richard made sure Janet was okay, and then he said they could enter. Monty and Spencer walked in.

"Darwin just phoned," Monty said. "They discovered some footage on one of Janet's neighbor's security cameras."

Both Janet and Richard were intrigued. "Capturing what?" Richard asked.

"Not a lot, unfortunately. Just a car near the beginning of the street Janet lives on. It showed a gray Chrysler 300 drive onto her street just after you arrived on that street, and then it showed it leaving a few hours later, after you had left."

"It was a gray Chrysler 300 involved in that ambush at the mill," Richard said, leaning up on his elbow.

"That's why I knew you would want to know," Monty said. "I remember you told me what kind of car was involved in the mill incident. Darwin remembered too."

"Was he able to track it down?" Richard

asked.

"He was," said Monty.

"Good. Where?"

Monty exhaled. "That car belongs to Doris, Richard," he said.

Richard's heart dropped. Because he suddenly remembered that Doris did drive a Chrysler. But he never even thought about her being involved. It was insane!

Janet was shocked too. "Doris, your secretary?" she asked Richard.

"His secretary," Monty said, nodding.

"His longtime secretary," Spencer said. "What you think, Richard?" he added. "All this shit could be about a woman scorned?"

Richard threw the covers off of him, revealing his pajamas. "Get ready, Janet," he said. "We're heading back to Tulsa." And Janet, in her own pajamas, began getting up too.

But Monty had reservations. "I don't think it's a good idea taking her with you," he said.

"Where I go," Richard said, "she goes. Get ready, Janet."

But Janet was already hurrying for the closet where her clothes were hanging.

"I'll get Fiona up," said Spencer, hurrying out too.

But Richard frowned. "Spence, I truly don't want to have to put up with that woman's bullshit right now."

"Where I go, she goes," Spencer said. "Just like you and Janet. And I'm going with you. For back up." And he hurried out.

Richard looked at Monty. "Just ignore her like I do," Monty suggested. "But you may need Spence's backup. He's going with you." Then he looked at Janet. "We'll keep Maurice here until I get the all-clear from you guys in Tulsa. Then he'll fly back on my plane."

Janet nodded. "Thank you, Monty," she said. "You've been very kind."

"My brother finally has the good sense to be with a good woman? It's my pleasure," he said, and left the room.

But as they put on their clothes, Janet was worried about Richard. Because he looked stricken to her. "How long has she worked for you?" she asked.

"At least a decade," Richard said, dressing quickly.

"I hate to ask it," Janet said, "but is there more to your relationship? Is that why she may be jealous of us, or something like that?"

But Richard was shaking his head. "Nothing like that," he said. "I never fuck anybody that works for me."

That was a surprise to Janet since he was willing to let her work for him. And they had most definitely fucked.

But she was more concerned about Richard's state of mind. "But a decade working for you?" she said. "It still has to hurt if she's involved."

Richard stopped for a moment, as if Janet had spoken the truth. His face was like an iron curtain of anguish. Because if it was true, and Doris was involved, it wouldn't just be a shame. It would be a betrayal too. Maybe the biggest, since she was his most trusted aide.

He continued getting dressed without saying another word.

Janet remained silent too.

CHAPTER THIRTY-THREE

The SUV stopped in front of the country home on a country road in Tulsa and everybody waited for Richard to make his move. It was late, just past midnight, but he just sat there, behind the wheel, looking at the quiet home and then at the road ahead of them.

Janet sat beside him, up front, but she dared not suggest he move it along. Spencer and Fiona sat on the backseat, and they were anxious for him to get on with it too. But they knew how close Richard was to Doris Wilson. They knew he didn't like this. At all.

And Richard was anguished. There was no other word for it. Was Doris jealous of his relationship with Janet? Could that be what it was about? He told Janet it couldn't be, since he never had a sexual relationship with Doris or anybody he worked with. But what else could it be? Doris was the one who set up their restaurant date for him. She was the one he ordered to arrange for that Mercedes to be delivered to Janet six years ago. Was she threatened somehow?

It seemed like a flimsy motive to him. But they all saw that video on the plane ride back to

Tulsa. And it was unmistakable. The Chrysler that had been at the mill and had fired shots at Richard and Janet, was the same Chrysler that was seen on Janet's street the night somebody had tampered with her brakes. They couldn't see the driver, or what happened when that car was parked. But they saw it come onto her street, and leave from her street, and the plates were undeniable. That car was registered to Doris.

He looked at Janet. He especially wanted her there with him. She was the one who could have died that day. He squeezed her hand. "Ready?" he asked her.

She wasn't sure if she was or not, but she nodded her head, anyway, and they all got out of the SUV.

With Spencer in the back, the two ladies in the middle, and Richard up front, they walked up to the front door and rang Doris's bell. Spencer was hypervigilant, looking around, making sure there were no surprises. And then Doris opened the door.

And she looked genuinely surprised. "Richard? What on earth are you doing here this time of night?"

"May we come in?"

"What's wrong?"

"May we?"

"Yes, of course." She was still confused, but she stepped aside and allowed them in.

"Are you going to tell me what's going on?"

"Where's your car, Doris?"

"My car?"

"Yes, your Chrysler. Was it stolen?"

Doris shook her head. "Stolen? Why would it have been stolen?"

Spencer and Janet both looked at Richard. He asked because, they knew, that was what he wanted her to tell him. That it had been stolen and she knew nothing about its whereabouts.

But she didn't tell him that. "It's in my garage," she said. "Why?"

"I need to see it," Richard said.

Janet could tell Doris wanted more information. She wanted her longtime boss to tell her what was going on, but she was used to doing whatever he told her to do. Even if it infringed on her right to say no. She escorted them through her dining room, and her kitchen, and then through the attached garage door.

And there it was: a gray Chrysler that looked just like the Chrysler in the video. Only the back windshield wasn't shot out the way Richard had shot out the Chrysler at the mill, and there were no bullet holes to be found anywhere else on the car either. And they all looked all around the car to be certain. No one found a single bullet hole.

"Who drives this car, Doris?" Richard asked her.

"You know I drive it," she said. "I've driven it for years. Did something happen that I don't know about?"

"Did you let somebody else drive it recently?" Spencer asked.

"No. Nobody other than Cary taking it to his shop for some ball joint repair work."

"His shop?" Janet asked. She also didn't know who Cary was.

"He's a mechanic," said Spencer, and Janet was immediately suspicious. Somebody tampered with her brakes and the guy who had possession of the Chrysler at least for some of the time happened to be a mechanic? She looked at Richard. Did he realize it too? Or was his hope that Doris wasn't involved clouding his view?

Which reminded Janet. "Wait a minute," she said.

Everybody looked at her. "What is it?" Richard asked.

Janet hurried to the back of the car. They all followed her. Then she saw what she thought she had noticed. "Where's the dent?" she asked, looking at the back of the car.

"What dent?" Richard asked her.

"That dent on the bumper. In those videos, the Chrysler we were seeing had a dent on the back bumper. On the right side of the bumper."

"You're right," Richard said, remembering too. "You are right."

And then, as if somebody had been listening from the kitchen area, a man appeared in the doorway. "Nobody invited me to the party," he said with a smile on his face.

Richard was surprised to see him. "Hello, Cary," he said.

"Good to see you again, Richard," Cary said, shaking Richard's hand.

"I didn't' know you were over here."

"I just drove up. What's going on?" he asked.

"That's what I wanna know," said Doris. "He's asking a lot of questions about my car."

"What kind of questions?" Cary asked. "Hey, Spence, good seeing you again."

"You, too, Cary. And you remember Fiona?"

"Yes, I do. How are you?"

"I'm good, thank you," Fiona said.

Then Cary looked at Janet.

"And this is my girlfriend, Janet," said

Richard. "Janet, meet Doris's friend, Cary Vance."

But even Doris seemed surprised that Richard would refer to Janet as his girlfriend. That was a first.

Cary was surprised too. "Nice to meet you, Janet," he said. "And welcome to the family. My lady has worked so long for the Shetfields that we feel as if we're a part of the family."

"Thank you," Janet said. She didn't know what else to say to that.

"They were just saying something about a dent," Doris said.

"That's right," said Richard.

"What dent?" Cary asked.

"On the back bumper," said Doris.

But Cary was shaking his head. "There was no dent on this car. Not that I recall."

But Spencer could tell that Doris disagreed. Richard saw it too. "You remember a dent being there?" he asked her.

"Yes. And on the back bumper like she said. I've had it for years."

Cary hunched his shoulder. "Oh well. I guess one of my guys buffed it out when I had it at the shop."

"Richard stared at him. "That could be it," he said.

"But why does it matter?" Cary asked. "What's wrong?"

Richard exhaled. "This car was involved in a couple of incidences involving me and my lady."

"What kind of incidences?" Cary asked.

"Bad incidences. The back windshield was shot out, and there should have been lots of bullet holes all over this car."

Doris was shocked. "Bullet holes?"

Cary smiled. "I think you have the wrong car, Mr. Shetfield. D's car was never shot up, at least not to my knowledge."

"We have video of that car involved in both crimes," said Spencer. "The tag belonged to Doris."

"I don't know how," said Cary. "Unless . . ."

"Unless what?" Janet asked.

"Unless somebody took the tag and put it on another car that's just like ours. Which could have been done the few days I wasn't at the shop. I have guys coming in and out all the time."

"But why would somebody do that?" asked Janet.

"To frame me," said Doris. "That's the only reason I can think of. But what would they be framing me for?"

"Or, they used Doris car," Spencer said. "That would explain why they buffed out that bumper, in case there were any videos taken."

"And they buffed it out after that windshield was blown out. They had to replace that too."

But Richard and Janet knew all of that was nonsense. How were they going to replace all of those bullet holes? They looked at each other.

"But what would somebody be trying to frame me for?" asked Doris. Then Doris realized what. "The brakes?" she asked Richard. "They wanted you to think I was involved in that brake incident."

"And the incident at the mill, yes," said Spencer.

"Oh, my goodness," Doris said. And she looked at Richard. "And you thought I might have had something to do with that?" She even looked shocked to Janet. And a little hurt too.

"It was a lead," Richard said. "We were just checking it out. But I'm glad there's nothing to it."

"So am I," said Doris. "Lord knows."

Spencer exhaled. "Let's get out of these good people's way," he said, and he and Fiona began leaving. Richard took Janet's hand, and they began leaving too.

At the door, they were saying their goodbyes. "See you tomorrow at work, Boss," Doris said.

And it was just about to be over. They were all heading out. Until Richard stopped in his tracks, forcing Janet to stop too. "What is it?" she asked him.

Richard suddenly realized what he was missing. That name. And those Italians at that strip mall. There was Bartoli. And Scapaletti. And Vance.

He looked at Cary. At Cary *Vance*. And without letting anybody in on his thinking, he pulled out his loaded pistol, and hurried over to Cary. And with screams from Doris, Richard kicked Cary's legs out from beneath him and dropped him, his back slamming down hard on the hardwood floor.

Spencer immediately pushed Fiona back inside and closed the front door. And pulled out his weapon too. He didn't understand why Richard was reacting the way he was reacting, but there was always method to Richard's madness.

Janet was shocked. What on earth was going on? But she knew Richard would not have done what he did unless it was vital.

Richard placed his gun to Cary's head. "That car in the garage? That's not Doris car, is it?"

Cary shook his head, nervously staring at the barrel of that gun. "No it's not."

"It's not?" Doris was floored. "What do you mean that's not my car?" She hadn't driven it since it was returned to her from his repair shop, but she had no reason to doubt it.

"What did you do to her car?" Richard asked Cary.

"Junked it."

"And you put the plates on a different Chrysler?"

He nodded. "Yes."

Doris was shocked. "You did what?" she asked her boyfriend. "Why?"

"Who are they to you?" Richard asked Cary.

Cary seemed terrified to Janet. "Who are who to me?"

Doris was terrified too. "Richard, what are you saying?"

"Who are they to you?" Richard asked Cary again. "Who are those three Italians to you? Tell me before I blow your motherfucking head off!"

"My brother!" Cary quickly yelled out. "One of them was my brother."

"Wait a minute," Spencer said. "Are you telling me that one of those three Italians at that strip mall was related to you?"

"Yes," said Cary, sounding as distressed as he looked. "They hired him and the other two." Then Cary yelled angrily. "And you killed them!"

"Their asses tried to kill us!" Spencer yelled back. "What the fuck did you think we were going to do?"

Janet was shocked to hear it. They killed some Italians at a strip mall?

But Richard was singularly focused. "What did they hire them to do?" he asked Cary.

Cary didn't respond.

Richard slammed his head into the floor repeatedly, yelling for him to answer his question.

And Janet was stunned. She knew Richard could be crude and rude, but she never saw him like this!

Richard hated that she had to see him showing his ass, but she was going to have to get used to it. And he didn't let up. This fucker knew who tried to kill them. He was never letting up. "Hired them to do what?" he angrily asked again. "Hired them to do what?!"

"To figure out a way to kill your ass!" Cary finally yelled back, unable to bear the pain another second.

And Richard did stop. But Spencer

looked at Richard. "Those Italians were there to kill you? We thought their asses came back gunning for us because they were angry with the way that meeting turned out."

"That's what they wanted us to believe," Richard said, "just in case one of us survived their ambush."

"But that meeting didn't have shit to do with it," Spencer said.

"Nothing," said Richard.

And Janet was in pure shock when she heard what they said. Somebody was hired to kill Richard? Richard and Spencer had to kill somebody or be killed? It was shocking. So shocking that she wondered what on earth had she gotten herself into. She thought whoever did her brakes, and whoever tried to shoot them down at the mill were women scorned. She truly believed it all had something to do with the fact that Richard was giving her some attention, and they didn't like it. She assumed that woman at the restaurant, that Margo, had hired somebody to take her out. Or some other woman she'd never met before. Or Doris when they got the word about her car being involved. She thought it was all about the women in Richard's life. She understood that kind of revenge. But to hear it had nothing to do with that? What was she getting herself into?!

Fiona leaned against her grinning, as if she could smell Janet's distress. "Get used to it," she said to her. "Especially with Richard. He's crazy."

But Janet didn't like anybody dissing Richard. She liked Fiona, but that little snide remark of hers rubbed Janet the wrong way. "He's not crazy," she quickly responded. "He's playing fire with fire. He not bringing a knife to a gunfight. I think that's the opposite of crazy." And then she moved away from Fiona.

But Richard was still digesting the fact that the Italians were involved. He thought he was helping out his brother. He thought it was as simple as calling a meeting to sniff out crooks and put them in their place. When those crooks were the ones sniffing him out. And tried to snuff him out too!

And Richard had to get to the bottom of it. For Janet's sake, he had to find out the who. "Who hired them?" Richard asked Cary.

"My brother didn't know. He said they never showed their faces. They handled it through text messages on throwaway phones. I told him not to do it. I begged him! But he did it anyway. Now he's dead."

"Okay, what's your excuse?" Richard asked. "Why did they hire your ass?"

Doris was shocked at Richard. "He had

nothing to do with that!" she cried. "You know Cary. He would never harm you! Nobody hired him to do anything!"

"What did they hire you to do?" Richard asked him, ignoring his longtime secretary. "And don't make me ask again!"

"To rig your woman's brakes," Cary finally admitted, crying too.

Doris was shocked. So was Spencer. Cary was supposed to be one of the good guys.

But Richard was confused. "Why would they want you to rig her brakes?" he asked.

"I don't know why," Cary responded. "They didn't tell me why. Everything was handled through my brother. I didn't even know he was dead until after that night, after I rigged those brakes. And we still haven't found his body. But I know you took him out. He was going to meet with you. And I haven't heard from him since."

But Doris was still stunned. "You were the one who tampered with Janet's brakes?" she asked Cary.

"What about that shooting at the mill?" Spencer asked.

"That wasn't me. I think they handled that themselves. I rigged her brakes. But that's all I did."

Richard looked at Cary. He couldn't

believe he said that. "That was *all* you did?" he asked him. "My lady came within inches of her life ending, within inches of colliding with a fucking train, and you have the nerve to say that's *all* you did?!"

And his control broke right then and there and he took that gun in his hand and began slamming it violently into the side of Cary's face like the thug he sometimes could become.

Doris was screaming because she knew how far Richard could go when he was angry enough. She knew his secrets. "Don't kill him! Richard, don't kill him! You're gonna kill him, Richard! Stop!"

But Richard didn't even hear her. He was down on his knees pistol-whipping Cary so violently that it sounded as if he was beating on a side of beef rather than a man's face. And Cary's face was caving, and all the bones were shattering, but Richard kept brutalizing him.

Janet didn't know what to do. She looked at Spencer. But Spencer was shaking his head. "He's getting what his ass deserves," he said. "He could have killed you when he tampered with your brakes. What you expect your man to do?"

Janet understood that too. But she was more concerned about Richard than getting revenge. "I expect my man to stay out of prison," Janet said anxiously. "That's what I expect my man to do!"

Spencer smiled and Fiona laughed. "Don't worry," Spence said. "No Shetfield will ever go to prison."

"And you can take that to the bank, honey," Fiona added.

And right then and there Janet realized she was in a different world now. In the world of the rich and powerful. In a world where scores were settled on the field, not in courtrooms. A world where, if anybody ever tried to harm her, Richard was going to handle it himself.

Personally.

It was as exhilarating for Janet as it was alarming.

But it was painful for Doris. She was crying and screaming for her boss to stop, but even she wasn't trying to physically stop Richard either. She'd lived in his world for at least a decade. Janet was certain this couldn't possibly be her first rodeo. She was crying because it was her man in the bullseye at the rodeo.

But Richard did finally stop. His gun was dripping with Cary's blood. Cary was already unconscious. He stopped. And Doris rushed to Cary's side as Richard stood to his feet.

Richard was breathing so heavily that he

could hardly speak.

Doris looked up at Richard with pain in her eyes. "Call 911. Let them call 911, Richard!"

Richard stared at her. "You had nothing to do with this?" he asked her.

"Me? Fuck you for thinking that I could do something to harm you! After all we've been through? Fuck you, Richard. Fuck you!"

Snot was coming from her nose and tears from her eyes. Janet could tell Richard was torn. He believed her, but he was angry that she was still trying to help the man who didn't try to harm Richard, but tried to harm his lady. He was defending Janet's honor, and her very life. She'd never been in that position before in her entire life.

And Richard gave in. "After we leave, you can call 911," he said to Doris.

She nodded her head. "Thank you."

"If my name or Janet's name or my brother's name is mentioned by him, you, or anybody else, I'll finish the job. And you know I will."

"My name too," said Fiona. "You better not mention my name either. Right, honey?" she asked Spencer.

"Yeah, right," said Spencer.

"And by the way," Richard said to Doris as he was about to turn away, "the police will be notified of his crime. They will be waiting for Cary when he arrives at the hospital."

Doris understood what that meant. Richard owned a lot of the cops on the Tulsa police force, especially the high-ranking ones. The fix was already in, and Cary was going to have to serve time for what he tried to do to Janet. But at least Richard wasn't making him pay with his life.

"Thank you for sparing his life," she said to him.

But Richard didn't want to spare anything when it came to Cary's ass. All he could think about was what that bastard tried to do to Janet. How she nearly collided with that train. The fear that was in her voice when she realized she had no brakes. All because of his ass.

And Richard couldn't take it. He went to the garage, looked around, and found what he could use. And then he returned inside the house with a metal baseball bat in his hand. And before anybody could even ask him what he was doing with that bat, Richard took it and slammed it into both of Cary's legs. Repeatedly. Until he was certain that Cary would never walk again.

Then he tossed the bat aside, and he and Janet, and Spencer and Fiona, walked on out.

When they got to the SUV, Spencer had

to drive. Richard was in no state for driving. Fiona sat up front with Spence.

Richard sat on the backseat, with Janet leaned against him. He had wrapped his bloody gun in his handkerchief, but she could see that his knuckles were badly bruised too.

"Where to, Boss?" Spencer asked his brother as he looked at him through the rearview mirror.

"The airport," Richard said, still trying to come down from that heavy lift he had to do in Doris house.

"Back to Texas?"

"Yes," said Richard. "Until I find out who else is involved, I want Janet out of harm's way."

And he kept his word. He phoned his contact at the police department, told him what Cary had done, and ordered him to meet Cary at the hospital. "Put his ass in cuffs at his hospital bed," Richard said, "and keep a guard on his door. I want to know everybody that comes near him. Especially any shady characters."

"What about Doris?" the high-ranking officer asked Richard.

Richard gave a hard exhale. "She knew nothing about it. Keep her out of it. But I want that fucker tried to the fullest extent of the law. I want him to do more years than he's got left on this earth for what he tried to do to my lady. Fuck it up, and you'll answer to me."

"Don't worry, sir. I'll handle it personally."

And the call ended.

Janet looked at Richard as Spencer drove them to the airport. "You believe her?" she asked him. She didn't want his emotions to cloud his judgement.

Richard leaned his head back. "She's been with me a long time. Through thick and thin. I have to believe her."

"And if you're wrong?" Janet asked.

"She'll get what's coming to her," Richard said. Then he looked at Janet, saw that she had too much of a window into his rotten soul, and he looked away.

A chill ran down Janet's spine. She was falling in love with a man who didn't just play, but played for keeps. You were either all in with him, or all out. She'd never met a man like him in all her life.

"I know my philosophy of life is hard to take," Richard looked at her again and said to her. "But that's how I was raised and I don't know any other way. I protect what's mine, and what's mine protects me." Then he smiled. "Including your gangster ass."

Janet was surprised. "Me?"

"I heard what you said to Fiona. About

not bringing a knife to a gunfight. That was some gangster shit you said right there."

Janet smiled.

"Mama Bear," he added, and they all laughed.

But Janet kept staring at Richard until he looked her way again. She was still smiling, but she was curious. "What kind of people are the Shetfields?" she asked him. "Are you businesspeople, or gangsters?"

Spencer looked at them through the rearview mirror. How would Richard answer that question? Janet already saw more than he would have liked her to witness. But Richard had total faith in her. And Spence had total faith in Richard.

Richard was still smiling when Janet asked him that question. But then his smile completely left. "Businesspeople when you leave us alone," he said. "Gangsters when you don't."

Janet nodded her head. That sounded completely logical to her, in a twisted, weird, billionaire kind of way.

"Can I ask you one more question?" Janet asked Richard. Spencer looked at her again through the rearview.

"You can ask me anything you like," Richard said to her.

"Does shit like this happen to you every day?" she asked him.

And Richard and Spencer and Fiona, too, all broke out in great laughter. Richard placed his left arm around Janet and pulled her close. "No, darling," he said, still laughing, "hardly ever."

But he also knew that when shit did come down, it poured like rain.

CHAPTER THIRTY-FOUR

But as if to make a liar out of Richard, within minutes of telling Janet that he hardly ever had such a string of problems the way they were having over the last few days, Janet received a text message on her phone with a video link. When she said the name of the video out loud, Spencer, who was driving them to the airport, nearly slammed on brakes. And he looked at Richard.

But Richard was looking at Janet. "What did you say?" he asked her.

"The name of this video link," Janet said, "is Pourtnoy. What in the world is Pourtnoy?"

But Richard and Spencer knew what it was. It was the name of an accountant that worked for Richard years ago. An accountant that had embezzled millions from Richard, and he handled him too. Spencer wasn't there when Richard handled it, but he'd heard all about it.

"Maybe she shouldn't open that," Spencer said.

But Janet had already pressed the button. Richard leaned against her, watching the video too, his knuckles still aching from that beat down he gave to Cary Vance. But this was different.

He knew as soon as the video came in focus and his old accountant was sitting in that chair. His head accountant, Myron, was seated beside him going down the list of offenses Pourtnoy had committed. And then the video showed Richard, who had been pacing the floor, pick up a rusty nail and shove it through Pourtnoy's eye. Janet almost dropped her phone when she saw Richard do that to that man.

She was floored. She looked at Richard. How could he justify such cruelty?

But Richard didn't skip a beat. "He embezzled millions of my money. He had to pay," he said. Then he looked away from the video, and into Janet's worried eyes. "I did what I had to do," he added.

Janet sat her phone on her lap. She was still stunned. "Did he die?" she asked.

Richard shook his head. "Not by my hands. I sent him to the hospital. Told him to have his ass back on the job when he recovered."

"Back on the job?" Janet asked.

"That's right."

"Even though he stole from you?"

"That's right," Richard said. "After that nail stick, I knew he would never steal from me again."

The logic, Janet thought, was foreign to her. But completely logical!

"But he never came back to work," Richard said.

"Did he pay you back?"

"Oh, yeah. He definitely did that."

"But the question is," Spencer said, "who the fuck sent that video to Janet?"

Richard had already wondered about that too. He took her phone and checked out the sender. It had just been sent. But by whom? "He has a handle, not a name," Richard said.

"What's his handle?" Spencer asked.

"Uncle K," said Richard. And then Richard froze.

Spencer caught it too. "Not that fucker," he said, glancing at his brother through the rearview while continuing to drive them to the airport. "I thought he was in prison," he added.

"So did I," said Richard as he pulled up Google on Janet's phone.

"Who's Uncle K?" Fiona asked, but they all ignored her.

But Janet wanted to know too. "Who's Uncle K?"

"Pak Kai-Shah," said Richard. "A con artist and a killer. A very nasty piece of work." Then Richard found what he was looking for.

"He was released a couple weeks ago," he said.

"Why would a person like that send me this tape?" Janet asked.

"Apparently he wanted you to know what kind of man you were getting yourself attached to," said Fiona.

Fiona had a point. Janet looked at Richard. "You think this Uncle K person could be the man who paid those Italians, and who was going to pay Cary Vance?"

Spencer looked at Richard through the rearview. "That's what it seems like to me, too, Dick," he said.

"But why?" Janet asked.

But Richard kept his own counsel. They all could tell he was thinking. And even Janet knew to leave him alone. He'd answer when he was ready to answer.

But he didn't say another word until they arrived at the airfield. Spencer stopped the car, and then he and Richard made eye contact through the rearview. And Richard nodded.

"Let's get out, Fee," Spencer said to his fiancée and he and Fiona got out of the SUV.

Then Richard turned to Janet. But Janet had already figured it out. "You aren't going with us. Are you?" she asked him.

Richard shook his head. "Can't. I need to find Kai-Shah or you'll never be safe."

"And what are you going to do when you find him?"

Richard wasn't going to lie to her. "Get him before he gets me," he said.

Janet sat there. And tears appeared in her eyes. "You be careful," she said to him. "I really need you to come back to me."

Richard smiled. "So you're all in now too?" he asked her.

Janet frowned. "Of course I am! You've risked your life to save mine. And if I didn't have you on the phone when my brakes had failed, if you hadn't phoned me, I don't know what I would have done. Of course I'm all in. But I was never the problem. Was I?"

Richard nodded. "No. You never were. But I'm no longer the problem. Okay?"

Janet nodded. "Okay." And she kissed him on the lips.

He tried to smile too. "I'll see you in Texas," he said, and they got out of the SUV.

Spencer and Fiona were waiting by the driver side door. Richard walked around to his brother's side. "Take care of her," Richard said.

"I will."

"She comes first," Richard said.

And although Spencer resented that, he knew it was true. Monty was at the top of the pecking order in their family, and Richard was a close second. Their needs and wants always trumped Spencer's. Now Richard expected him to protect Janet even over Fiona. He had some balls!

But Spencer knew his brother was going into harm's way. He wasn't going to give him something more to worry about. "I know," he said to him.

And then Spencer, Janet, and Fiona made their way toward the plane. Janet kept looking back at him. He kept waving at her.

And then he got behind the wheel of the SUV and watched Janet as she headed for that plane. He was falling hard for her. Super-hard! All those wasted years when his dumbass could have had her by his side. He was going to make up for lost time.

But first, he thought, as he pressed the Start button, he had to find that crazy-ass Uncle K.

But just as he was about to put the SUV in gear, he realized something he had seen. On Janet's phone. That video had just been sent to her, just before they made it to the airport. As if Uncle K saw when they left Doris house. As if Uncle K knew where they were heading next. As if Uncle K was one step ahead of Richard just as those Italians he hired were too!

Which meant, Richard said out loud, and

then he realized what it meant. And he looked as Janet and Spencer and Fiona were about to walk up the steps of his plane.

And he jumped out of the SUV, pulling out his gun, and running toward them. "Don't get on that plane!" he was yelling at the top of his lungs. "Don't get on that plane!"

Spencer was the first to hear him, and then Janet and Fiona heard him too. And they all heard the panic in Richard's voice.

Spencer was already pulling out his weapon, but even he was too late.

The man Spencer and Richard immediately recognized as Pak Kai-Shah, better known as Uncle K, came out of the plane with a loaded assault rifle in his hands, and fired as soon as he appeared. Fiona took a shot straight through the head and fell straight backwards, even as Spencer was grabbing her and Janet and pushing them aside. Even as Spencer was trying to shoot back. Even as Richard stopped running, aimed his own weapon, and took his best shot at that motherfucker, aiming straight for the heart. But that was after Uncle K had already aimed at Spencer and Spencer took a shot to the stomach. And fell to the tarmac too.

But Richard's aim was dead-on. Uncle K, seemingly stunned that he had been hit at all, fell over, down the steps of the plane, and onto the tarmac. He landed on top of Fiona.

Richard ran to the foot of those steps. He ran as fast as he could run.

Janet had run to Spencer, removing her jacket to compress his bleeding stomach wound, but he was waving off Richard, who ran to him too. "Fiona," he said. "Help Fiona!"

Richard grabbed Uncle K's dead weight and threw him aside. And that was when he saw Fiona. A gunshot through the head. There was no way she survived that. He looked at Janet. And shook his head.

"Is she alright?" Spencer was asking them. "Is she alright?"

But Richard was already distracted. He saw movement from Kai-Shah. And he aimed his gun at him. But first he needed to know why.

"It was my money," Kai-Shah was saying. "He stole it because I ordered him to. He stole it to set me up for the day I walked out of that prison. Took me six years after you killed him. Because you killed Pourtnoy. He was my sister's only son and you killed him! They said he committed suicide. But that was a lie. I knew it was a lie. You killed him. You made him give all that money back and then you took him out. And as soon as I walked free, I declared I was gonna make sure I took you out. And everybody you loved too."

"But it didn't work, did it, asshole?" Richard said. "I'm still here. And so is my brother. And so is my woman. You failed again you miserable sonafabitch! And for the record, I didn't kill him." And when Kai-Shah tried to reach for Richard's gun in one last attempt of vengeance, Richard shot him one time, through the heart again. And that was enough. He was dead.

Then Richard went to Spencer even as they heard sirens in the distance. The air traffic controller at the small airfield had apparently phoned 911, and then got out of the way.

"There's nothing more we can do but wait on the ambulance," Janet said. "Go check on your crew on the plane. Make sure there's nobody else trying to come for us."

It was Richard's thought as well, and he began running up the steps onto the plane. When he saw that his flight crew had been gaged and tied up, rather than killed, he sighed relief. And made sure nobody else was on that plane.

Once satisfied, he untied his pilot, who would untie the rest of the crew, and then Richard ran back to aid his brother.

But when Spencer finally found the strength to lift his head up and look over at his fiancée, and saw the state she was in, he began wailing in despair. He cried like a baby.

And Richard had to hurry down to him, and hold him, even as they saw the police cars and ambulance on the tarmac heading their way.

Janet continued to apply pressure, even though they both knew it was no use. He was bleeding profusely. It would take a miracle.

But they had managed to come together again, despite the incredible odds. They both believed in miracles.

EPILOGUE

"Said the shepherd boy to the might king,
'Do you know what I know?'
In your palace warm, mighty king,
'Do you know what I know?'
A child, a child, shivers in the cold,
Let us bring him silver and gold.
Let us bring him silver and gold."

The Regney/Shayne Christmas carol *Do You Hear What I Hear* hummed softly in the background as Richard, Janet, and Mo celebrated Christmas together at Janet's house. It was snowing very lightly outside, but Richard had never felt as much warmth and closeness as he felt inside his heart.

His family was celebrating Christmas at their individual homes in Texas, and although Spencer was out of the hospital and recovering nicely at Monty's house, he was still in a state of grief over Fiona and didn't feel like celebrating anyway. Fiona was a pain in the neck most times, Richard knew, but she had a big heart too. He hated what happened to her. He hated that he didn't figure it out in time to prevent it. But he understood grief. He knew Spencer's heart would recover. But Spencer needed time to grieve.

But Richard wasn't going to let anything spoil Christmas for Janet and Mo. They had enough of life intervening and spoiling their happiness. Not this Christmas.

But he needn't worry. Mo, being Mo, wasn't about to let anybody spoil his Christmas. They were eating, but Mo was speeding them along like an excited child.

"Alright now, we need to hurry it up," he said again. "We got to leave to get to the arena in time. And this is a lot of food we got to eat."

Richard laughed. "Don't worry, Mo. We're going to sit in my skybox. We won't have to wait in line."

Mo was surprised. "We won't?"

"Not for a second," Richard said.

Mo smiled. "Well alright! I'm liking you more and more boy."

"Oh, Mo," Janet said. "Just because he has season tickets to every Thunder game and owns a skybox is enough to gain your like?"

"It sure helps," Mo said with a grin.

"Although," Richard pointed out, "neither one of you are supporting the Thunder on this beautiful Christmas day."

"Not when LeBron's in town, we aren't," said Mo. "But any other time? We're down with

Oklahoma. LeBron's in town? Bump Oklahoma! What they ever did for me?"

Richard and Janet laughed. And Richard looked at her. Thanks to her, all three of them wore matching bright-green ugly sweaters, but Janet, he thought, looked radiant in hers. "This meal is delicious," he said to her. "The best Christmas meal I've ever eaten."

"He lying," Mo said, and Janet laughed.

"I'm not lying," Richard said, trying to keep a straight face.

"It's good," Mo said. "Don't get me wrong. She makes a mean potato salad. But the best ever? I don't think so! But y'all hurry up, now. And we got the gifts to open too? And we got to drive an hour and a half to get to the arena? We gon' be late for sure. I wanted to see LeBron warm up!"

"We'll get there on time," Richard said. "We aren't driving. We're flying over to Oklahoma City. We'll get there in no time flat. Stop worrying so much."

Mo smiled. He knew he could go overboard. But he felt like a kid again. He felt like he had anything he wanted at his fingertips, and he wanted it all!

But they did manage to get through the meal and settle around the Christmas tree, where the gifts were. Mo had the lion's share, plenty from Richard and Janet. And he couldn't wait to get started.

"I'm use to one gift for Christmas. A tie and a hundred dollars from Janet."

"Why the hundred dollars?" Richard asked.

"Because she knew I was gonna take that tie back to the store and get what I wanted. The hundred dollars was just extra in case what I wanted cost more. I get that every year."

Richard looked at Janet. She smiled. He was dressed in jeans with his ugly sweater, but to Janet he never looked better. "It's our Christmas tradition," she said. "We wanted to establish one, and that became it. I got Mo a tie and gave him a hundred dollars, and he went and took it back and got whatever he wanted. I did it the first year he moved in with me, and when he took it back, I told him I won't get him a tie ever again. But he said get him one every Christmas. He like taking it back. He like getting that hundred dollars. It became our tradition."

But this year, Mo had designer suits and shoes and anything and everything. "I'm gonna enjoy taking all this back," he said happily, and Richard laughed.

But then it was time for Richard to open his gifts. Janet had gotten him a beautiful smoking jacket. "It's gorgeous, babe," he said, and kissed her.

Mo had gotten him some psychedelic socks. "To go with my ugly sweater?" he asked Mo.

"No you didn't say that," Mo said, and they all laughed.

And then it was time for Janet to open her gifts. A pair of psychedelic socks from Mo, and a huge box from Richard.

"Look like a mink coat in that thing," Mo said.

But when Janet opened it, no coat was inside. Just the tiniest of boxes. A jewelry box.

Mo stopped everything. His heart almost stopped too. He looked at Janet.

Janet was having palpitations herself. But she didn't want to get ahead of herself. She didn't want to embarrass herself if it wasn't what it looked like it was.

It was what it looked like it was because Richard took the box from her hand and got down on both knees at her chair. And then he opened the box.

"Damn!" Mo yelled when he saw the size of that rock. "I ain't never seen no diamond that big in my life!"

"I've never seen a diamond in my life," Janet said, stunned.

"Me neither," said Mo. "That's what I

mean."

But Janet was too shocked to pay Mo and his doublespeak any mind. She wasn't even staring at the ring. She was staring at Richard. "Traditionally," Richard said, "you're supposed to take a long time to ask a lady to marry you. But I feel as if I've waited six years. Six long, lost years. I'm not waiting another day."

He moved closer to her chair. "Janet Felicia Evans, will you become Janet Felicia Shetfield?"

Janet couldn't help it. Her whole life flashed in front of her. All the putdowns and disgusted looks. All the tear downs and hopelessness. Last called for basketball. Never even invited to anybody's ball. Now she was the belle of the ball? And Richard wasn't just asking to be her date, but to be her husband? She broke down crying unlike she had ever cried before.

But Mo was scared her hysterics were going to scare Richard away. "Yes!" he yelled. He was in tears too. "I've prayed for this moment. Yes! She says yes. And so do I!"

Richard laughed heartily. He finally knew what it meant to be in a happy family. And this was his family now, Mo and Janet, though not in that order. "I appreciate your vote of support," he said to Mo, "but I think she has to say it herself."

"Oh, yes," Janet said between her cries. "I will marry you, Richard Everhouse Shetfield."

Mo stopped smiling and looked at Richard. "Everhouse?" Mo said.

"And will you have my babies?" Richard asked Janet.

Janet sighed. She could not believe how much it would be her pleasure to have his children. "Yes," she said. "And I will have your babies."

"Our babies," Richard said.

Janet nodded, smiling this time. "Our babies."

And then they both stood to their feet and embraced.

"Everhouse?" Mo asked again, still unable to figure out that stupid name. But he looked at them, and he was smiling too.

> *"Said the king to the people everywhere*
> *'Listen to what I say.'*
> *Pray for peace, people, everywhere.*
> *'Listen to what I say.'*
> *The child, the child, sleeping in the night.*
> *He will bring us goodness and light.*
> *He will bring us goodness and light."*

Visit
www.mallorymonroebooks.com
or
www.austinbrookpublishing.com
or
amazon.com/author/mallorymonroe
for more information on all titles.

ABOUT THE AUTHOR

Mallory Monroe, a pseudonym of award-winning, bestselling literary author Teresa McClain-Watson, has well over a hundred bestselling books under her name. They include MaeBelle Marie, the Alex Drakos Romantic Suspense series, the Oz Drakos series, the Reno Gabrini (Mob Boss) series, the Mick Sinatra series, the Sal Gabrini series, the Tommy Gabrini series, the Big Daddy Sinatra series, the Trevor Reese series, the Rags to Romance series, the Teddy Sinatra series, the Boone and Charly series, the Monk Paletti series, the President's Boyfriend series, and the President's Girlfriend/Dutch and Gina series. She has also worked as an executive editor for many years and as an investigator for three. Recently widowed, she has attended Florida State University, Florida A & M. University, the University of North Florida, and the University of Mississippi at Oxford Summer Law Institute. A law school dropout, she holds a Master's degree in history and education and credits God Almighty for ALL of her success.

Made in United States
North Haven, CT
23 December 2022

30077426R00207